FINESSIN' A THUG'S HEART

JAMMIE JAYE

Finessin' A Thug's Heart

Copyright © 2021 by Jammie Jaye

All rights reserved.

Published in the United States of America.

All rights reserved. No part of this publication may be reproduced, distributed, or transmitted in any form or by any means, including photocopying, recording, or other electronic or mechanical methods, without the prior written permission of the publisher, except in the case of brief quotations embodied in critical reviews and certain other noncommercial uses permitted by copyright law. For permission requests, please contact: www.colehartsignature.com

This is a work of fiction. Names, characters, places, and incidents either are the products of the author's imagination or are used fictitiously. Any resemblance of actual persons, living or dead, businesses, companies, events, or locales is entirely coincidental. The publisher does not have any control and does not assume any responsibility for author or third-party websites or their content.

The unauthorized reproduction or distribution of this copyrighted work is a crime punishable by law. No part of the book may be scanned, uploaded to or downloaded from file sharing sites, or distributed in any other way via the Internet or any other means, electronic, or print, without the publisher's permission. Criminal copyright infringement, including infringement without monetary gain, is investigated by the FBI and is punishable by up to five years in federal prison and a fine of $250,000 (www.fbi.gov/ipr/).

This book is licensed for your personal enjoyment only. Thank you for respecting the author's work.

Published by Cole Hart Signature, LLC.

Mailing List

To stay up to date on new releases, plus get information on contests, sneak peeks, and more,

Go To The Website Below...

www.colehartsignature.com

1

KRESHA

"I fucking hate his ass," my cousin Maci cried out. She had just found out that her longtime boyfriend Lee was cheating for the millionth time. I didn't know when she was going to stop letting him make a fool of her. She knew better, they had been going through this for as long as I could remember. He would cheat, and she would stupidly take his ass back. I knew that she had to be tired of his shit because I was, and he wasn't even my nigga. Niggas like him were the reason I was single. There was no way that I was going to let a nigga play with me. The last relationship that I was in taught me that niggas were not to be trusted. A nigga can tell you that he loves you all day, but as soon as he gets mad or walks out of the house, all that shit goes out the window.

"It's gone be ok, boo." I assured her as I rubbed her back. I was tired of hearing about this shit with him, but I would never tell her that. I was her backbone, and she was mine, so I would always be there for her. I knew that when she was tired of his shit, she would stop fucking with him. She deserved someone that would love her the way that she needed to be loved. At twenty years old, we should have been going out and enjoying life, but that was the last thing that either of us were able to do.

We had goals to accomplish. We both were in school and working.

My Grandmother died a few months ago. That left us devastated. She seemed to be in good health, but when *it* hit her, it hit hard. It broke my heart, I guess in my mind I thought that she was going to be here forever. I wanted her to see me walk across that stage. This fall was going to be our senior year. We had been taking summer classes since I had gotten out of high school so that we could be finished in three years.

"I just can't believe that he would do me like this again. "I'm done crying over his ass," she huffed before getting up and wiping her face. I just looked at her knowing she had said this shit a million times. Lee was a big distraction for her in my eyes. She was slacking in school, and she knew that we had a plan to be done with college in three years instead of four. I was going to school for accounting, and she was majoring in art. We had goals, and there was no way that I was going to let her fall off worrying about his ass.

"Look bitch, you are beautiful and smart. There is someone that will love you the way that you need to be loved. Fuck Lee. It's time for you to boss up and show that nigga what he is going miss out on. I'm not going to let you get down when we have so much to be happy about." I knew that she was going to get mad, but I didn't care. Just as the thought occurred, she glared at me and walked out of the room, meaning that she was mad. I didn't follow behind her. I sat on my bed and picked my phone up. I scrolled on Facebook until I scrolled past a picture of my ex that had been posted by his brother saying that he was coming home soon. Just seeing a photo of him made me mad. Every time I saw his face, I would think of all the heartache and pain that he put me through. If I could kill his ass and get away with it, I would. That ruined my mood for social media, so I closed the app and got on TikTok. I didn't want Nell on my mind at all. He was a thing of the past.

I got comfortable on the bed because I knew that I was

going to be on TikTok for a while. I was off work for a change, so all I planned to do was chill. It would have been nice to go and shop, but I had goals I was trying to accomplish.

"Yo' Mama said that she finna go to work and to make sure that Pops take his medicine," Maci advised as she walked back into the room. I looked at the time and realized that my ass had been on TikTok for a few hours now. "She be acting like he handicap," I fussed. My grandfather was just fine. It seemed that after my grandmother passed, my mother started babying him.

"Girl let that lady do for her daddy," Maci said as she flopped down on the bed. I hated when she did that. At this point I felt that she was doing it because she knew that it would make me mad. She had been doing it all our lives. Maci had been living with us since high school. Her mother was in the Army. Since she was never home, she had Maci move in with us, and when she came home she stayed here as well. My grandparents had been in this house for as long as I could remember. We lived in the hood, but our house did not look like it. It was well maintained. My grandaddy made sure that his house was good. I was just happy that he was still here with us. He wasn't doing bad, but my mama liked to baby him like he was unable to take care of himself. That man could do all the things that she could do.

"You know that we gone get past this together," I assured her. I wanted her to know that I had her back. My ex had broken me down to my lowest point, so I knew just how she was feeling. He had me feeling like I never wanted to be in a relationship again. Hell, I never wanted to be loved again in the way that he loved me. No matter how much I tried to stop thinking about Nell, I just

I Imagine couldn't. I knew that he was going to make shit hard for me. Why couldn't he just let me live my life and be happy? He treated me like shit, so I didn't get why he couldn't just leave me alone. Nell was selfish as fuck. He had been in jail for a few years so my life had been okay, but I knew that as soon as he got out, he was going to come and try to hurt me in any way that he could. I wished that they could keep his ass there forever. I knew that at some point that I was going to have to face him. I just wasn't ready right now. I didn't need the distraction.

"Let's walk to the store," Maci suggested, breaking me from my thoughts. I didn't reply and instead got up so that I could change. I was still dressed from earlier when I went to apply for a job. I had a day job at a call center, but I needed a little more money coming in so that I could pay for extra classes. I didn't get student loans because I didn't want to be in debt my whole damn life. I thought about being a bottle girl at the club that Maci worked at, but I wasn't sure if that was for me.

I slipped on a cute fitted Maxi dress and some slides and grabbed my wallet as we headed out the door. The neighborhood was popping, there were people everywhere. I hadn't ever seen it like this, but this was the first weekend of the summer. I remembered back when I was in high school, the beginning of summer break was always lit. Sometimes I wished that I could go back. It's crazy that our parents always told us that we needed to stay kids as long as we could. I believe that shit now.

"Well look who's outside," my homegirl Star said sarcastically. It had been a while since the last time that I saw her. She used to live down the street from us, but when her mother passed, she moved away. My girl was looking good, and I was happy to see her ass.

"Girl, we come outside," I joked back. She was right though. We didn't come outside often because we were always busy with work and school. I missed having fun. It had been so long since I had gone out and had fun. As I began to think about it, I realized that the last time that I had been out was for Star's birthday two years ago.

"Bitch, I been coming over for the past week and haven't seen y'all asses. I saw yo' mama the other day, but she was leaving as always. I didn't see your car, so I knew that yo ass was at work," she said confidently. That made me smile. I really didn't think that she thought about us.

"You know we got to get this money, friend," I told her as we leaned on her car. She was riding a nice Benz. Star and her boyfriend had been together for some time now. You could see the glow in her face, and I was all for happiness. Just like me and Maci, she had been thought some shit with her ex, so I wanted that for her.

"Where y'all was headed?"

"Girl, to the store so that I can get something to drink and some cigars," Maci told her as she texted on her phone. I knew that she was texting Lee's no-good ass. I prayed that he didn't try and come back around.

"Come on, I'm walking with y'all," she said as she locked her car. That made me think about old times when we were younger. The three of us were inseparable. You didn't see one without the others. Life just happened, so we lost touch. I prayed that we could get back to that point. I wanted to get back to living life and not just working.

We walked to the store and got what we needed. By the time we got back to her car, there were more people out. The walk was about ten minutes there and back, so I was shocked. When we walked back up the block, there were all kinds of things happening, bouncy houses were being put up and shit. My curiosity was interrupted by a group of females that walked past us. They looked a mess. There was no way that we would be caught looking like that.

"What they got on?" Maci asked, taking the words out of my mouth. I had no idea what they had going on, but I knew that I would never walk outside dressed like that.

"I forgot I seen that flyer about this block party. I saw it a few days ago, but didn't realize that it was today," Maci said before I had a chance to ask. I knew that I worked a lot, but I checked my social media often and I hadn't seen anyone post anything. At least I didn't think I had.

"Girl, Reese brother Jimbo just got out girl, so they are doing it big for that nigga," Star informed us. I just nodded. I knew who Reese was because he had been trying to talk to Maci's ass for a while. She was so stuck on Lee that she never gave him a chance. I didn't know that Reese had a brother. I knew that Star was with his cousin, but that was it.

We chilled until they started blocking off the street, she didn't want to be blocked in, so she parked at our house, and we walked back to the projects. It was nice to be able to just chill.

"Girl, Reese so damn fine," Maci said, shocking me. She was so loyal to Lee's ugly ass that she never really looked another niggas way. I damn near broke my neck looking at her to see was she serious. I had never heard her talk about a man other than Lee.

"What bitch? Damn, I can't say the nigga fine? I mean I am a woman, right?" she rolled her eyes. Just as I was going to reply, a blacked-out G wagon pulled up in front of us. We were across the street from everything, sitting on the green power box, so now the truck was blocking our view. I was ready to shoot off until the door open and the finest nigga I had ever seen got out of the passenger seat. He was tall as fuck. His dreads were neatly styled, and that line was crispy as fuck. His Balmain jeans fit him just right. I can't lie, I was stuck. Then the way that he was licking his lips had my shit dripping.

"Reese, why the hell you park right here, blocking our view and shit?" Star questioned pulling me from my thoughts. Reese came around the truck, and when he saw what she was talking about he laughed and got back in the truck and moved it. When he got back out, they started talking, but I had no idea what the fuck they were saying because this nigga had my attention, and I knew I had his because he was doing the same.

"Take a picture, it will last longer," Star blurted causing us to stop looking at each other. I looked down at my phone, embarrassed. He just smiled, causing me to blush.

"Star don't make me call Lo on yo' ass. Do Cuz know you out here?" he asked her.

"Jim, stop it. You know he knows where I'm at," she informed him. The whole time that he was talking, I tried to distract myself with my phone, but that was not working. I could feel somebody looking at me, so I looked up, and Maci's ass was looking upside my head.

"Girl what?" I question. I knew that she wanted to say something about how I had been looking at him. I usually prided myself on not getting involved with any nigga. That shit was a big distraction.

"Nothing," she laughed. I knew it what it was, but I left it alone.

"Where that nigga at, anyway?" Reese asked as he leaned against the truck. '*Shit*,' I thought. '*My ass has been missing out, cause these some fine ass niggas*'.

2
MACI

"He on the way," Star told Reese. This man was so handsome. Reese had been trying to talk to me for a while, but I was loyal to Lee so there was no way that I would cheat on him. As if Lee could feel that I was thinking about another nigga, my phone rang. I hit ignore like I had been doing all day. I was done with his ass. I had said that a million times, but I was *done* this time. I knew that I deserve to be treated better than he was treating me. Lee was my heart at one point. I thought that I was his as well, but as time passed, I realized that wasn't the case. He had cheated more times than I could count. I stayed in hopes that one day he would change, but that never happened. I didn't tell Kresha, but he had gotten another bitch pregnant. I was so fucking embarrassed that I couldn't even physically say the shit. I was done with his ass, especially since he made me have an abortion with my baby because he claimed that he "didn't want any kids right now".

The crazy thing is, the nigga swore that the bitch was lying, but I didn't see why she would lie like that. A while back he told me that he was moving because his mama's house was getting foreclosed. He said that he was moving in with his cousin. Every time that I tried to come to see him, he would say that his cousin didn't like people coming to her house. I should have known then that he was with the shits, but I was so in love that I believed his ass. This nigga played me, but that shit was over.

"You better stop looking at me like that before I show you what it's like to be with a real nigga," Reese smiled. I really didn't even know what the hell to say. I was accustomed to turning him down that I had to think about my response. Just as I was about to reply. I heard Lee's ass call my name. Reese just looked at me and shook his head.

"Let me know when you ready to fuck with a real nigga," was all that he said before walking off. I sighed and walked to see what he wanted. I didn't want my girls to hear us because then they would know what his ass had done.

"What do you want, Lee?" I asked as I walked up to him. As soon as I was in arm's reach, he pulled me close to him. Before, that would have made me smile, but now I was disgusted. I didn't want his ass to touch me.

"Why you talking to that nigga?" he questioned as if he had the right to. I didn't deny it because I knew that I had been talking to him. He was standing in front of me, but he had has spoken to me first. Lee didn't want me to talk to anyone but him.

"Lee, why are you here?"

"Baby, I keep telling you that she is lying. That bitch is not pregnant by me," he lied. I just looked at his ass once again. There was no reason to argue back and forth with him. I had done enough of that over the past three years. Like Young Miami said, "I am not about to be drunk and stressing over a piece of man that's not mine". She could have his ass because I now knew that he wasn't worth shit. I didn't know why I stayed this long. That shit wasn't for me, hell *he* wasn't for me.

"Okay, so she lying about you living with her too, right? No, *you* are the one that's lying. Lee I'm done. You fucked up, now you gotta live with that. Go and be with her because clearly she makes you happy," I expressed, waiting on his ass to lie. He dropped his head and that was all that I needed to see. I pulled away. There was nothing more to say. I walked off and left his ass standing right there. He chose to cheat, so he was going to deal with the consequences.

When I made it back over to Star and Kresha, they were smoking. As soon as I sat down, Kresha passed me the blunt. I needed it. We sat and chilled on the green box while everyone partied. It had been so long since we had done this. I missed it. Life had happened so damn fast that we never had time to just chill. I went to school three days a week, worked at Nike in the morning, and as a bottle girl at this strip club called Streetz at night. I had goals that I wanted to accomplish, so I did what I had to do. I was actually thinking about not doing summer classes. I just hadn't told Kresha yet because I knew that it would disappoint her. But I was drained. I needed to take a break. I was twenty and had no life. She would always say that the hard work would pay off. I didn't doubt that, but I knew that I could never get these years back, and neither could she. Hell, she worked a full-time job, had just applied for a part-time job, and did small marketing jobs on the side.

"Hoe, what you are thinking about?" Kresha asked me.

"Nothing."

'Girl please we been talking to you and yo' ass ain't heard shit," Star said. I hadn't heard shit, but I wasn't ready to tell her what was on my mind. It wasn't the time or the place. I would tell them when the time was right.

"I guess," Kresha said. I knew that they both knew that I was lying, but they didn't say anything. They just let me be great.

"Can I talk to you or yo' nigga gone pop back up?" Resse questioned. He had me blushing just from saying that. He smelled so fucking good that he could talk to me about anything. The way that he was invading my space had my shit wet.

"You can talk to me whenever you want," I assured him. I was single now, so it was free game at this point. He grabbed my hand and pulled me to him. Out of the corner of my eye, I could see that Lee's cousin was looking at me. I didn't care though. I wanted to throw this shit all in his face. He needed to see that he had lost when it came.

"So, when you gone let a nigga take you out, and show you how real niggas do?" he questioned.

"When you got time, you know you a busy man," I added. I couldn't lie, it would be nice to actually date someone. Lee never took me out. There were so many times that I asked him to take me out, and he swore that he was too busy getting money. I was glad that I was done with that chapter in my life.

"What you doing later?"

"I have to work later."

"Where you work?"

Don't get me wrong, I'm not ashamed of where I worked but I didn't really tell people. I didn't have time for the judgment.

"Ummm, I work at Streetz as a bartender at night and Nike during the day." He just nodded. A part of me wanted to know what he thought. We stood around and talked until it was time for me to head to the house. I really didn't want to go, but I needed the money. Him and Jim ended up walking us to the house. Star decided to just leave her car at our house, and she got in with her man. Kresha and Jim took a seat on the porch. Since I had to work, I headed in the house and Reese headed back to the park.

As soon as I walked in, I laid back on my bed and closed my eyes. All I could think about was the heartache that I was going through. Why did this have to happen to me? Why couldn't he just love me right? I knew that this was a part of life, but that didn't make the shit okay. I rubbed my hand down my flat stomach thinking about the baby that previously grew there. It had only been a month since I had the abortion. I should have known when he let me go through that shit alone that he didn't give a fuck The fucked-up part was that Kresha didn't even know about the baby because soon as I found out and told him, he told me that he didn't want any kids because he was in the streets. I went through all that he was out here having babies with other bitches.

My phone rang, pulling from my thoughts. I looked down and saw that Lee's name was flashing across the screen. I just shook my head and silenced the call. I didn't want to hear shit that he had to say. I placed my phone on DND and grabbed my clothes so that I could take a shower. I had a little over an hour until it was time for me to go to work. I showered, went to check on my grandfather, then I went to talk to Kresha. When I walked into her room, she was on her phone smiling, so I knew that she had to have been texting Jim's ass.

"What's up bitch, you ready to tell me what's on yo' mind?" she asked as soon as I walked into her room. I sighed and sat down on the edge of the bed. I dropped my head because I knew that she was going to mad and disappointed at me.

"It's a few things Kresha. I really don't know where to start. I know you gone be mad, but I have to tell you before I fucking go crazy," I couldn't even get the words out because of the tears that were flowing. I took a moment to think of what I wanted to tell her first.

"Aw boo, tell me what's wrong. You know I hate when you cry," Kresha said as she sat next to me and pulled me in for a hug. This the kind of moment that I needed my mother in, but she wasn't there, as always. I hated that she cared more about work than she cared about me. She had been in the army before I was born and soon as I was old enough to do things on my own, she was gone. She only came home twice a year. I need her to be a mother to me.

"Kresha, I just can't do all of this. I think that I want to take the summer off. It's just too much. Then there is Lee. He is the biggest issue. He made me have an abortion then I found out that he got someone else pregnant," I cried. She didn't say a word, she just hugged me, and that was what I needed at the point. We talked until it was time for me to go to work. It felt so good getting it off my chest.

"Maci, can you take these bottles to VIP?" Dawn the other bartender asked. Dawn was the only female that I really talked to at work. She was cool as hell; the rest of these hoes were fake. They had it bad, fucking each other's niggas and shit. I didn't rock like that at all, so I kept my distance.

"Okay," I replied grabbing the bottles then heading to the VIP. I had been working here for a while now. This was where I met Lee's dog ass.

Tonight was extra packed, as was any Friday. I walked to the VIP and waited on security to unlock the gate. As I walked in my eyes landed on Reese. A smile instantly graced my face. I gained my composure and headed toward him with the bottles. Once the sparks went out, I sat the bottle down and walked off. Before I could get far, he grabbed my arm and pulled me back to him. The smell of his cologne had me ready to drop to my knees right then.

"Remember that you not gone be working here that long. I don't need these niggas look at what's mines," he whispered in my ear before letting me go. I didn't respond, I just walked off. What was understood didn't need to be explained. As I made it down the small set of stairs, Lee's ass appeared from the hall that lead to the bathrooms. I rolled my eyes and kept walking because I didn't want to be bothered with his ass. I knew that he was going to start some shit. Once I got closer, I saw that he was so into his phone that he didn't see me, and I was happy about that. I made my way back to the bar so that I could help Dawn knock down the crowd that she had.

The night flew by, before I knew it the club was clearing out. I normally worked until everyone was gone, but today that was not happening. As soon as the bar closed, I headed to the back to get my shit. Once I had everything, I went to the manager to tell him that I was gone and that I would just get my tip-out tomorrow. When I knocked on the door, he yelled for me to come in. I was not expecting to see Reese's ass in there with him.

"Um, I was just letting you know that I was leaving and that I will get my tip-out tomorrow," I said in a hurry. There was something about the way that Reese was undressing me with his eyes that made me nervous.

"Okay, cool. This my cousin, Reese. Reese, this is-"

"Maci," Reese finished his sentence.

"Aw, I guess y'all already know each other then. I'm moving to Atlanta, so he is buying the place from me," Cal explained. I knew my ass was going to have to find a new job because there was no way that I could be around his ass every day. "He is taking over in a few weeks. Don't tell anyone else because they don't know yet." Cal was a cool older guy. He wasn't a creep like most club owners. I never heard of him messing with the girls, and he didn't allow that drama shit. He would fire a motherfucker in a hot second.

"Okay well, I will see you tomorrow Cal." I closed the door and headed out. When I made it to my car, Lee was leaned against it. Why didn't he get the picture? He needed to just move on. There was no way that I could forgive him. If I did, I would have been making that shit cool, and it wasn't.

"Lee, what is it?" I asked as I unlocked the door to my car.

"Maci, you really tripping, you know that a nigga loves you." I knew that was a lie, but part of me wanted to believe him. Lee was so damn fine. Plus, he was getting his money in the streets. That didn't matter because I now knew that he didn't deserve me. I didn't matter how fine he was or how much money he had we were done.

"No I'm not nigga, you made me kill my fucking baby just so you could go get another bitch pregnant. I'm done Lee, you may as well go and be with her because I'm over this and you. I gave you too many chances. I forgave you for all your fuckups. The hurt that I feel right now I will never forget. At this point I don't see why you don't get it."

"Maci when do you have time for a nigga? You always working or at school. You weren't ready for a baby."

"So, because I want to make something of my life, I'm wrong? That has to be the dumbest shit you ever let come out your mouth."

"What you doing all of that for? I got you. I been telling you that. Maybe if you would have made the time, we could have had a baby," he stupidly said. I just shook my head because there was nothing more to say. He had lost his fucking mind. He was always blaming me for his fuckups. My dumb ass was always taking the blame, but not this time.

"Okay, Lee. You right it's all my fault. We know that, so can you move so I can go home? I'm tired," I told him as I got in my car. Once I was in, he stopped the door so that I couldn't close it. He just looked down as if he was expecting me to have something else to say. His ass was going to be waiting forever. I was done. After he saw that I was not going to say anything, he backed up.

"Just know this shit forever and if you think I'm going to let you go, you can forget it," he said before kissing my forehead and closing the door. I started my car and pulled off. What he said didn't matter because I knew this was over.

3
REESE

"Is she a good employee" I asked Cal soon as she closed the door. Maci knew that I wanted her ass in the worst way. I saw that she had a nigga, and I didn't have time to be beefing with no nigga over his bitch. Now that they were no longer together, she was going to be mine.

"She cool and keep away from the drama. The nigga that she used to fuck with is the problem though. That nigga makes sure if she is at work, he's here," he informed me. I just nodded. I wasn't worried about her nigga. One thing for sure, no nigga put fear in my heart. I knew the nigga from the streets, so I knew that he was not about that life.

"Well, I'm heading back out here. You know Jimbo ass out there lit, and I would hate to have to kill a nigga about my brother," I explained. We shook hands and I headed to get my brother out of here. We had just finished discussing the plans to hand everything over. My brother had been home for a few days, so playtime was over. It was time to get this money up.

When I made it back to the VIP, he had two females next to him while Lo sat back watching on his phone. I'm sure his ass was texting Star ass. Lo ass was in love and that was some new shit. Lo was the dog of all dogs, shit that nigga was the one that taught *me* the game. So seeing him in love gave a nigga like me hope.

"Come on bro," I called out so that he would know that I was ready to go. He got up with both females holding on to his ass like he was going to leave them. I just shook my head. Lo walked behind them and I walked in front. It wasn't that my brother could handle himself, but he was fucked up. He wasn't a drinker, but this was his second day home, so he wanted to celebrate.

Before walking out the door, I checked to make sure everything was good. I knew that we had enemies in the streets, and I didn't need a nigga trying to get one-up on us. Even though my brother had been gone for five years, nothing went through this city without our approval. We had been running this shit since our father was killed. Our father Mill was killed by his right hand Dru, which is why I don't trust any nigga other than my brother and cousin. After Dru killed my father, he stayed around. It wasn't until he found out that we knew it was him that he disappeared. To this day, I was still looking for that nigga because I was going to kill his ass just like he killed my father.

I waited until my brother and his hoes got in before I jumped in the driver seat and Lo got in the passenger seat. Jim was staying at my house until his house was finished getting built. I had booked him a room because there was no way that these hoes were going to know where I laid my head. Just as we pulled up to the hotel a text came through.

Trin: what's up yo haven't heard from you in a few days.

Trinity was my lil jump-off. She was cool, just not the girl for me. She didn't have any ambition. Her folks had money, so she didn't want to work hard for shit. She had some good pussy though, so she would do for now. Plus, she was fine. Thick ass thighs and a small waist. I didn't get how someone so pretty could be so okay with the little that she had.

Me: I will be through in a minute
Trin: ok

"You need us to walk you up?" I asked Jim as they got out. That nigga laughed and lifted his shirt showing his gun. I just shook my head and watched him to the door. Once he walked in, I pulled off heading to drop Lo off. The whole way there my mind was on Maci's fine ass. I was going to get her ass. I just needed to make sure that she was done with that nigga. I didn't want to have to add to my body count if I didn't have to.

I pulled in his gate and Star ass was standing at the door waiting. I couldn't do shit but laugh. They were funny as hell, but I loved that shit. I couldn't wait to have that kind of love. A nigga was getting older, and I wanted kids and shit. I loved my niece and nephew, but I wanted my own kids to spoil. Hell, I wanted a woman to spoil.

"Aye nigga, be safe," he said as she got out of the car. I dapped him up. He closed the door and I pulled off. I headed straight to Trinity's house. She lived in a nice ass condo downtown that her daddy paid for. One thing that I did like was that she never asked me for anything. Not that I wouldn't give it to her, but shit it was nice to keep my shit in my pockets. All the other females that I fucked with kept their hands out. When I pulled into the parking garage, I pulled next to her Beamer and called to tell her that I was on the way up.

"Hey baby, I missed you," she greeted me soon as I walked in the door. She only had on one of the t-shirts that I had left and panties. Just seeing her fat ass hanging from under the shirt hand my dick rock hard. I kicked my shoes off and followed her to her bedroom. This was always the routine. We fucked and I dipped.

"Show me how much you miss me," I demanded as I took my clothes off. As soon as my pants hit the floor, so did she. I really didn't care for her head, it was basic as hell. She didn't have any special tricks, she just sucked it. The crazy thing is she thought that she was really doing something. I let her do her thang until my shit started going soft. I then pulled her up and place the condom on my dick as she crawled in the bed. She loved getting hit from the back and I loved doing it.

"Throw that ass just like that baby," I moaned out. She was moving just like I liked, but for some reason my mind was on Maci.

"Umm baby, I miss this dick so much," she cried out as I damn near broke her back. I really wanted her not to talk because I was imagining that she was Maci's fine ass. Just the thought of her had me ready to nut. I was trying to hold it, but I could not. Soon as I felt my nut coming, I pulled out.

"Damn you must really miss me, baby. You never nutted that fast," she said causing me to laugh. She was right, but it had nothing to do with her ass. I quickly got dressed so that I could go home. I didn't even clean my dick off. I did not need her thinking that it was going to be something that it wasn't. I fucked up and did that before.

"Resse, when is it going to be more than this? We been fucking for two years and never went on a date or shit." See, this was the shit that I was talking about. She wanted more than I was willing to give so, I knew that I needed to fall back. I didn't even give her the pleasure of a reply. I finished getting dressed and walked to the door. I could hear her talking shit behind me, but I didn't care about any of that shit. As soon as I walked out the door, I blocked her number.

She was doing the most. One thing that I was not about to do was let her make me feel like I had to be with her. Plus, she thought that I didn't know that she was fucking with other niggas. She was saying that we had been fucking-off for two years as if that would change anything. I jumped in my car and headed to the warehouse that we used to house all of our inventory. I wanted to make sure that everything was good because we had a shipment that had just come in. I liked to come at night because it was quiet. We dealt with everything from weed to guns. There wasn't much that we didn't have our hands in.

As I walked around, I reflected on how well shit had been going. Outside of this street shit, we had so many business deals going. My goal was to be a billionaire. I had long ago made it to millionaire status. There was nothing that I wanted that I couldn't have. My brother, my cousin, and I made sure that the whole family was good. I mean, there were a few exceptions but for the most part, we all were good.

Once I made sure everything was good, I headed home. When I walked in the door, I looked at the clock and saw that it was five in the morning. I headed to the shower then straight to bed. I knew that tomorrow was going to be a long day.

JIM

I was happy to be a free man. I had been waiting a long five years to get my freedom back. The day that I got locked up, I just knew that they were going to find my ass. Normally my workers do pick-ups, but some shit had gone down so I did it that day. Lucky for me, my father had the police chief on payroll because he was able to help a nigga out a little. If we didn't have him, they would have put a nigga under the jail. That shit set a nigga back, but we bounced back and moved differently now.

I had been watching these two bitches fuck and suck on each other for the past hour. I hadn't fucked them because one of their pussies was stanky and I couldn't figure out who it was. There was no way that I was going to take a chance with that shit.

They were cool with fucking each other, so I chilled and smoked. For some reason, my mind kept going to Kresha. Lil mama vibe was so cool. I can't lie, a nigga didn't want to leave her earlier. I had offered for her to come out with me tonight, but she said that she was good. Outside of thinking about her, my mind was on getting my money up. My brother and I had purchased the club Streetz as well as a few apartment buildings.

I wanted to have some shit to fall back on if something ever happened. I wanted some shit to pass along to my kids other than a drug empire. Honestly, I didn't want my kids in the streets at all. But I knew that I had no power over that. I want Lil Jim to do something big with his life and Miya could just be daddy's little princess just like she was now.

After I was tired of watching them, I told them they could have the room for the night, and I headed out.

I didn't have plans to be there all night, so I had dropped my car off before we went to the club. It was almost four a.m., so I decided to roll through the hood. I wanted to see how shit was rolling at night. Since I had been gone, my brother had changed shit around, so I wanted to see how it was working out. My brother felt that I need to chill for a minute, but that was not going to happen. I need to get back to the money. Yeah, I had money, but I wanted more. I needed to get this money and get out of the game. I didn't want to go back to jail or get killed in these streets. I had two kids to take care of. This wasn't something that I wanted to leave for my kids. I wanted to leave legit business.

While I was locked down, I came up with a plan so that I could be done with this shit in two years max. I wanted a better life for me and my family, and I was going to make that shit happen. As I rode the streets, I thought about what I needed to do to get this shit in motion. I knew that it wasn't going to be easy. There were too many niggas out here that felt that like they were doing big shit, so I knew for sure that someone was going to try me, and I was ready.

A smile graced my face as I pulled up to the block. Shit was rolling just like it needed to be. I rode around the block a few times before putting my brother's address in the GPS. It didn't take me long to get to his house. I made sure that I had everything that I needed before I headed into the house. As soon as I got to the room I was staying in, I fell asleep.

Ring Ring!!!

I woke up to my phone ringing off the hook. When I picked it up, I saw that it was my baby mama Shae. I rubbed my hand down my face because she was finna run me the fuck crazy. She had been blowing my ass up since I had been home. I went to her house the first day that I was out, and she acted like she was my bitch not wanting me to leave and shit. Shae knew damn well that what we had was dead.

"What's good Shae?" I answered. It was like she was calling just to be calling. She didn't want shit, just wanted to talk. I had heard that she was out here wildin' while I was gone. As soon as she got around me, she started acting like she was doing the right shit while I was gone. I guess she didn't realize that niggas in jail knew what was going on before niggas on the street did. She was fucking the city, and that shit was foul because she was a nigga baby mama. It was way too many niggas out here that could say that they had what should have been mine, so I was good on her.

"I need you to get Ja'Miya," she damn near yelled. I wondered if something had happened with her but chose not to ask. It wasn't my business, plus that was my baby, so I was not going to question her about getting her. There was no reason to trip. I never understood how niggas didn't want to get their kids. There was nothing more important than them, not even money. All that shit could wait when it came to them.

"Aite, I will be there in a little while," I told her before hanging up in her face. I threw the phone across the bed before throwing my legs off the bed. She just wanted to run the streets. The whole time that I was gone she was putting my baby off on my mama. I knew that my old lady didn't mind, but that wasn't the point. She was a mother and needed to act as such. All her ass did was party. I had been hearing a lot of shit about her. I just hadn't addressed it because I knew that all she would do was get mad.

I jumped in the shower and got dressed before heading to get my baby girl. I had been gone her whole life, but thanks to my mother she knew who I was. My mother made sure that she brought her to see me every week. That was some shit that I would forever love her for. When Shae figured out that I didn't want to be with her, she wouldn't bring her. It was cool because I didn't need her ass holding shit over my head. Shea was a user, and I was not about to let her use my ass. She would have felt like I owed her something because she brought my baby to see me.

When I made it to her house, she was on the porch with her friends. I walked past all of them like their asses didn't exist. I didn't like half of them, and the others I didn't know. She was always hanging around new bitches. I didn't get that shit at all. That only showed me that she couldn't be trusted. My baby girl jumped up as soon as she saw me walk through the door. She was always happy to see me. Hell, I was always happy to see her. My baby was the female version of me. The only thing that she got from her mama was her hair. Shae was beautiful, she just was fucked up in the head. She had a body that would make the strongest nigga weak. Her yellow skin was filled with tattoos. If she carried herself right, she could have any nigga that she wanted. She was just small minded.

"Her bag over there," she told me as she stood by the door. I couldn't deny it, she was looking good as fuck, but I knew that she was not to be touched. That shit would open a door that I didn't want to go through. I didn't need her thinking that she had a chance.

I picked my baby and her bag up before walking out the door. I noticed that there were a few suitcases at the door, so I guess she was going out of town. She had her car seat on the porch, so I placed her in the car before going back to get it. I could feel those thirsty ass hoes looking at me. I made sure my baby was good and headed to my mama's house. On the way there, I called my son's mother to see if she could drop him off. I wanted to spend a little time with them before getting in the streets.

"What's up baby daddy," she answered.

"You busy?"

"Naw at the house, what's up?"

See, Kayla was the opposite of Shae. She never gave me any problems and she was a damn good mother. I never worried about my son because I knew that she was raising him right. She made sure that he knew who I was. That shit meant the world to me. Kayla was a good girl.

"Can you bring Lil Jim to my mama's house? I just picked up Miya, I wanted to spend some time with them. I will probably keep him until tomorrow."

"Okay, I will be there as soon as I get him together. I will call when I'm on the way," she told me before we ended the call.

My mama hadn't seen them in a few days, so I knew that she was going to be happy. Miya slept peacefully the whole ride to my mama's house. Every chance that I got, I looked back at her. God truly blessed me when he allowed me to get back to my kids. I loved them so much. There was nothing that I wouldn't do for her. As soon as the car stopped in my mother's driveway, she jumped up smiling like she was never asleep. I couldn't do shit but laugh.

"Nanna!" she screamed. I smiled gratefully. I helped her out of the car then watched as she ran to the door. By the time I walked in, she was outside in the back yard. I placed her bag on the stairs and walked into the kitchen where my mother was standing at the stove. My mama cooked every day like she had a house full of people. I thought that she would have stopped since I was gone, but my brother said that she never stopped.

"What are you cooking, beautiful?" I asked as I kissed her on the forehead. My mother was short as hell, so I had to bend down and kiss her.

"Cajan Pasta. You know yo' damn brother always asking for something," she fussed. I just shook my head and sat at the table. I made sure that I sat so that I could see my baby. The house was gated, but I still could never be sure. There were some sick people in this world. As she played, I just watched. My mama had so much for her to do in the backyard. I was thankful for my mother because she had held shit down for me and my kids. What she didn't know was that I was going to spend the rest of my life thanking her.

"Kayla finna bring Lil Jim. I gotta handle some shit with Resse then I'm going to come back and get them. I think we are going stay here tonight," I told her. She just smiled. That was something that she loved. If she could have us still living here, she would. She was so upset when she found out that I was staying with my brother until my house was finished.

Since I was waiting on my brother, I decided to chill with my baby girl and watch Frozen. My brother ended up coming shortly after I got there. Just as we were about to eat, Kayla called and said that she was at the door. I had seen her since I had been home. The first day that I came home, my mama had already had my son and I wasn't here when she picked him.

When I opened the door, my mouth dropped. Kayla looked amazing. I knew that she told me that she had gotten her body done, but damn I didn't expect what I was seeing. Before I left, she didn't have any ass.

"What's up daddy," Lil Jim greeted me pulling my attention from his mama.

"Whats good son?" I said dapping him up. He swore that he was a big boy. He dropped his bags and ran to my brother soon as he saw that he was in the kitchen, leaving me and his mother alone.

"Damn Kay," I said looking her over again. She didn't reply, she just pulled me in for a hug. When she pulled away, I could help but kiss her fine ass. I just knew that she was going to push me away, but she just blushed.

"Don't start no shit, Jim."

"My bad. I couldn't help it, you looking good baby mama," I admitted. She knew that I was an affectionate nigga. I liked for my bitch to show me that she loved me.

"You looking good too," she smiled. Damn, I knew that staying away from her was going to be hard. Kayla was a niggas first love. I was just on some other shit when I was younger. I was running the streets, not thinking how it would affect her. When she found out about JaMiya, I knew that shit broke her heart. She didn't talk to me for a long time. It was to the point that she would send my son with my mother most times.

"Well, I'm going to get out of here, just call me when you ready for me to come and pick him up," She told me as she walked off. I could help but look at her ass.

"I'm going to bring him home," I told her. I waited for her reply because that would let me know how far I could go with her. I just wanted a reason to go to her house. Hell at this point, I was going to come back tonight when the kids went to sleep. I watched as she walked off. A nigga dick was rock hard. I didn't really like that she had gotten her body done, but damn that shit looked good on her.

"Ok." I just smiled as I walked into the house. I couldn't wait to hit that pussy.

5

KAYLA

Seeing my baby daddy brought back feelings that I didn't even know were still there. Jimbo was that nigga back in the day and seeing him just told me that hadn't changed. That nigga was my everything at one point. I just knew that he was going to be my husband. He just fucked up and had a baby on me and that was some shit that I never thought that I would be able to get past. It hurt me to the core. He fucked me up. To this day I had trust issues. I had dated a few niggas, but it was like I always compared them to his fine ass.

One thing that I could respect was the fact that he never let the fact that he was in jail get in the way of him being in his son's life. Lil Jim never wanted for anything. Hell, I never wanted for anything. I worked because that was what I wanted to do, not because that's what I had to do. He made sure that I was good.

As soon as I got in the car, I called my cousin Trin. I couldn't wait to tell her what had just happened. I knew that she was going to clown me because I swore that I was not going to let him get in my head. Jim was the king of that. His ass knew what to say and do to get me to act just how he wanted. He knew what he was doing when he kissed me. I was not going to get involved with him, especially since I had a nigga. I knew that if my boyfriend Marco knew that I had let Jim kiss me, he would kill my ass. Marco was my baby. He was a street nigga just like Jim, but they were on two different levels.

Before I could call her number, my phone rang. I looked at the dashboard and saw that it was Marco's ass calling.

"Hello,' I answered.

"Where you at?" he questioned. I knew that he was just calling because he knew that I was going to Jim's house. I had told him that that I was headed there, so I knew that he was going to call.

"On my way back home, Co," I said with an attitude because he was doing too much.

"Pull up on me," he demanded.

"Okay," was all I said before ending the call. I really didn't want to pull up where he was because I knew that it was going to lead to us getting into it. He had been tripping since he found out that Jim was coming home. The nigga had asked to ride with me earlier when I was dropping my baby off. I knew that shit would have gone left fast. Jim didn't even know this nigga existed, and I wanted to keep it that way. The nigga had even tried to move in when he found out that he was coming home. I shut that shit down so fucking fast. That was not gone happen. I liked my own space.

It didn't take me long to get to him since I was already headed that way. When I pulled up, I called and told him that I was outside. I parked in front of the house that he was at and placed the car in park. I hated coming over here. I remember Jim used to tell me that the trap was no place for a woman. I sat there until I saw him walking out the door. I moved my purse to the back seat as he approached the car. I made sure that my phone was on vibrate because I didn't want it to ring while he was around.

"So, what's up with you?" he asked as he closed the door. I knew then that he was about to be with the shits.

"What you mean?" I asked.

"Why you smell like that nigga?" I just looked at him. I mean I did hug Jim, but there was no way that I smelled like him. Well at least I didn't think I did.

"Co, cut the shit. You must be having a bad day?" I asked, trying to get to the bottom of what the fuck was really going on with him. Just as he was about to answer me, his phone rang. He hit ignore before looking back at me. I knew then that it was a bitch calling. That was our biggest problem. Co wanted to be with me and any other female that wanted his ass but didn't even want me to look at another nigga.

"Why you hit ignore, Co?" I questioned.

"Because they can wait." This nigga thought that I was crazy. I knew that was a hoe calling his phone, but I wouldn't dare let him know that it bothered me.

"You trying to change the subject. You have been all over that nigga. You smell just like him. I knew I should have ridden with you," he said confidently as if it made sense. There was no way that I would have allowed him to ride with me. Jim would kill my ass if I would have brought that nigga to his mama's house.

"That's what you called me over here for?" I asked. He just wanted to make a big deal of nothing. He just wanted to make it look like I wanted Jim. Now don't get me wrong, I did, but that wasn't for his ass to know. Co needed to have the same energy that he had had for the past few months. He came around when it was convenient for him. I was cool because I didn't like to be all under a nigga any way.

He drilled me about him for a while longer until his phone started back ringing. We said our goodbyes, and I headed home. Since my son was gone, I decided to get some cleaning done. I wanted to make sure that the house was good because I knew that I would have to work some overtime. I didn't have to because Jim always made sure that I was good, but it was nothing like having your own money. Just as I was finishing up, my phone chimed.

Lil Jim Daddy: where you at
Me: at home
Lil Jim Daddy: ok I'm headed over there.

I couldn't contain my smile. There was just something about Jim. I knew that he was no good for me, but seeing him brought back all the love that I thought was gone. I sat my phone on the bed and headed to the shower. I wanted to make sure that I was smelling good just like he liked. I wanted my baby daddy back and I was going to get him. I just needed to figure out what I was going to do about Co. In a perfect world, I could have them both.

By the time that I finished showering, Jim was calling saying that he was outside. I stood by the door and waited. When I saw that Lil Jim wasn't with him, I got a little nervous.

I stood at the door and waited for him. I was dressed in some shorts and a tank. I had gotten my body done a year ago, so my shit was right. I knew that was why his ass was here. I saw how he had been looking at me.

"Why are you standing in the door?" he asked as he walked up. I just smiled and walked off. I knew that he hated that. As soon as the door closed, he pulled me close to him. He smelled so fucking good. I could just smell his fine ass all damn day and night. I had my face in his chest, but I could feel his ass looking down at me. I was short as fuck, so he was towering over me.

"You miss a nigga?" he asked as he kissed me. My damn panties were soaked. It was crazy that he had that effect on me.

"Just a little," I lied. I missed his ass like crazy. See, while he was gone, I really didn't have to see him, so I didn't know that I still had these feelings but being in his arms made it crystal clear. I had never felt like this about Co. Honestly, he was just something to fill the void, but I started to like him after we started to kick it.

"Show me you miss me," he told me. I stared at him. He just wanted to me suck his dick. It was cool though because I was planning to do that anyway. I walked him to my room, and as soon as the door closed, I began undressing him. He just stood there watching me letting me do my thang. When I pulled his pants down, his dick damn nearly smacked me in the face. As I sat face to face with his big ass dick, my phone started ringing. I knew that it was Marco, but he was going to have to wait. I saw Jim look at my phone and smile. He went to reach for my phone, so I rammed his dick in my mouth. I didn't want these problems. I knew that he wasn't a hoe ass nigga, and neither was Marco. I didn't want them to be beefing.

"Fuck," he moaned out. I made sure that his dick hit my tonsils. I wanted to make sure that this shit was like crack to him because I needed him coming back for more. I needed to secure my spot in his life. I doubted that he was fucking with anybody since he had just come home.

After he fucked my brains out, all I wanted to do was lay down. While he went to take a shower, I laid in bed thinking about what I was going to do about him and Co. I got up so that I could find something to put on. Just as I was walking into the bathroom, someone texted his phone.

Kresha: hey wyd

He was new to iPhones, so he didn't know how to change the settings so that his messages wouldn't preview on the screen. I had no idea what his lock code was, so I placed the phone back down.

Seeing that made me decide to keep Co around for just a little while longer. I did not want to get ahead of myself.

6
JIM

"Ummm," I heard from behind me. When I turned around, she was standing in the doorway. She was still naked. That shit had a nigga dick back hard. I wanted to fuck her thick ass again, but I had some shit that I needed to do. I didn't want to get distracted, but I had to see if the pussy was still good.

"What that mean?" I asked as I slipped my pants back on.

"Baby Daddy, you still looking good, and you still know just how I like it," she cooed as she got on her tiptoes to kiss me. I couldn't do shit but smile. She pushed past me, enticing me to look down at her fat ass. I bit my lip trying to contain myself. I had shit to do, so I couldn't get into all that with her. She knew just what she was doing. I slipped my shirt on before grabbing my gun and other shit off the dresser. I walked to her mirror so that I could make sure I looked good. As I adjusted my clothes, she hugged me from the back like she used to do when we were younger.

"I got your back like you got my front baby," she spoke, making me smile. This shit was crazy being here like this. It brought back memories of when I had first started hustling. She held a nigga down.

I turned around so that I could look at her. Kayla was so fuck pretty. It was not often that you saw a female that pretty.

"Ima be back later, or I might just have you come to my house," I told her as I towered over her. Seeing that smile on her face made a nigga day. I missed that shit.

"Okay just let me know baby," she said kissing me. I pulled out some money and placed it on the dresser as I walked out of the room.

As soon as I got in the car, I called Resse back. When he answered, it sounded like he was at the club. I looked at the time, confirming my thoughts. "Yo', pull up," he yelled. I ended the call and headed that way. The whole ride there, I smoked and thought about my plans. Life was about to change for me and my family.

I pulled to the front door of the club and got out. I really wasn't dressed to be clubbing. I liked to make sure that I looked good any time that I was out. I grabbed my gun and weed before getting out of the car and handing the valet my keys. I really wasn't on board with this club shit, but my brother swore that it was a money maker. The line was long as fuck, so he may have been right. I walked to the door and watched the thirsty ass females. I didn't bother to stop and say shit to security because they knew who I was. The club was packed. I headed straight to the office area. As I walked through, I made note of shit that I wanted to change.

The place was cool, but I wanted it to be an experience coming here. I wanted our shit to stand out. As I walked through the club, I scanned the room. My eyes fell on Kresha. She was in a section with Star's ass. I watched her as I made my way that way. I needed to go and talk to my brother, but I wanted to speak to her first. She had her back to me at this point, so I walked up as close as I could behind her. I wanted her to feel my presence. It took a few seconds, but she turned around. She smelled so damn good. The frown that she was rocking looked sexy on her.

"Why you all on me like that?" she asked.

"Damn I can't be close to you?" I asked as I pulled her in my arms. I looked her in her eye and that shit had a nigga lost. She was so fucking beautiful. Her hazel eyes had a nigga in a daze. So was wearing red lips stick, and the only thing that came to mind was what her big ass lips would look like around my dick. I know I was a fucked-up nigga to be thinking like that, but it was what it was.

"Nah, how you know I don't have a man?" she questioned as she pulled back from me. I knew that she didn't have a nigga. I had already been asking about her. There was something about her that intrigued me. She had this cool vibe about her. I liked that she was not half-dressed like the rest of these hoes in here.

"Do it look like I care if you have a man? I'm trying to be your man," I insisted. I knew that I had to have her. She didn't know, but I was a boss nigga, and I got who and what I wanted. There was no question about that.

"Well, looks like lil mama over there thinks different," she added, gesturing to me to look up and see my baby mama Shae. She was standing near the VIP door looking like she was mad. I didn't see why hell she was mad, but one thing I knew was that she was about to start some drama that I didn't have time for. Shae knew that I hated people to be in my business.

"I will be right back," I told her before getting up. I made my way over to Shae. I grabbed her arm and pulled her towards the office area. When I turned around her friends were following.

"Yall can go back that way," I told them, causing them to stop in their tracks and turn around. I knew they were the ones that had encouraged her to try and crowd me because she knew better than to do that shit. This was a club, but also my place of business. I opened the office door and Resse was standing at the desk. As soon as he saw her, he walked out. I needed to get her ass in line, or she was going to make shit hard for me.

"Yo, you just forgot that you have a daughter?" I questioned. She knew that I didn't play about my baby.

"Nigga I been had her. Yo' ass been in fucking jail. I need a break like you had a break. Besides, you in here all in bitches faces when you should be home with her," she slurred. I could tell that she was drunk as shit.

"You sound so fucking dumb Shae. I was in fucking jail, you think that I wanted to be there?" I yelled. She was acting dumb as fuck. Sometimes I wondered how the fuck I got her ass pregnant. My baby wasn't a mistake but fucking with her was.

"You need to chill out with all this partying. You need to make her your main priority, or she can just say with me," I told her ass. I knew that would get her attention, at least I thought it would.

"Better for me," she said before walking out of the office. A part of me was mad, but I knew how she was, so it was to be expected. Now I was going to have to talk to my mama because she was going to have to help me with my daughter. Once I got my mind right, I called my brother to tell him he could come back to the office. As soon as he walked in the door, I told him what had happened. His dumb ass just laughed like something was funny. I wanted to curse his ass out, but I just let him. One day he was going to have some drama and I was going to do the same thing.

7

RESSE

I had been in the office for a while watching the cameras with my brother. When we took over, we got a state-of-the-art system installed. We wanted to see everything that was going on. I should have been watching what was going on, but my focus was on Maci's pretty ass. I had been watching her for a while. She was good at her job. I was happy when I found out that she was done with that nigga. He didn't deserve someone like her. She was giving me a hard time but knew that she wanted me just like I wanted her. She was going to be all mine.

I sat on the couch listening to my brother tell me about his powder-head baby mama. I couldn't see how his ass didn't see it. I had been hearing it in the streets. Since he had been wildin', I knew for a fact that he was gone kill her ass when he found out. It was not my business to tell.

I made my way to the bar so that I could fuck with Maci. She was working the bar alone tonight. When she saw me walking up, she smiled as she handed the customer the drink that she had just fixed. A few people were waiting, so I helped her clear them out. Once we cleared the crowd, I walked closer to her and pulled her close to me. I could tell that me being close to her made her nervous, I thought that she would have been passed that point by now.

"What's up, beautiful?" I asked, kissing her on the neck.

"Reese, I'm at work. Why are you doing this? And you know how these hoes get about you, I don't need to be beefin' about a nigga that's not mine," she added. I smiled. She knew that I didn't care about the shit that she was saying. I didn't want any bitch in this room but her.

"I don't care about that shit. You not gone be working here long anyway," I told her. There was no way that my woman was going to be working like this. All I wanted my woman to do was spend my money and fuck me.

"What does that mean, Reese?" she asked. She knew exactly what the fuck I was saying. And if she didn't, then she was going to see it. I knew that my folks said that she was a good employee, but I was going to fire her ass. She stepped back and looked at my ass like I had two heads. I just smiled and pulled her even closer. She smelled so fucking good, which was saying something because we were in the club and there was smoke everywhere.

"Soon as Kim comes, I need you to meet me in my office," I told her before kissing her on the forehead and walking off. As I made my way back to the office, I saw Shae and her friend headed to the door. I shook my head because I knew that my brother had sent her ass on her way. I knew that soon she was going to be a problem. She was way too wild.

I walked into the office and focused on the camera. I couldn't help but to watch her. It was as though when she was around, she was the only thing that I could think about. I was at work, so I needed to focus. I pulled my thoughts away from her and looked at the papers that were on my desk. I had so much that I needed to get done. There was so much that I wanted to change. The way that he had it may have worked for him, but it was a no for me. I wanted this to be a pleasant experience for every customer.

I made a mental note to have everyone to come in for a meeting once I got shit in line. Right now, it was a strip club, but I wanted to be a strip club as well as a night club. The place was huge. There was so much room that he didn't make use of. The upstairs area was not being used at all. That was the area that was going to be the strip club. I knew that some of the girls that worked there were going to be mad because once I made the changes, they would not be dancers. Some of them needed to rethink the profession they had chosen. I wanted nothing but bad bitches. When I was done, this would be the hottest club in the south. We planned to change the name and all.

As I went through the papers, there was a knock at the door. I knew that it was Maci. "Come in," I called out. As soon as I did, the door opened, and she walked in. I stared at her.

"Why do you be looking at me like that?" she questioned as she took a seat on the couch. "This place looks so different."

When we took over, I changed a lot of shit. I wanted this to be a peaceful place, plus there was no telling what had been on the furniture that had been in here. My mama came in and redid the room so that we both would be comfortable.

"Thanks," I replied as I walked over to her. I wanted to be as close to her as I could.

"So, what are we?" she asked as she adjusted herself on the couch. I knew that I shouldn't have been at her like this knowing that she just got out of a relationship, but I didn't care about any of that shit. I wanted her and she was going to be mine.

"Damn you gotta ask that?"

"I mean you ask questions that you want to know the answer to," she expressed. Her ass knew just what the fuck I was talking about. I liked that she was playing like she didn't know what the fuck was going on. Her asking that shit let me know that not just any nigga could get her time. I knew that if she was hard on me, that meant that another nigga wouldn't have a chance. I could tell that she was nervous, and that shit had me laughing on the inside.

I pulled her to her feet so that I could hug her.

"Why are you acting like you don't know that you mine?" I asked as I watched the cameras.

"I don't know because you haven't told me. This is new to me."

I know that you have been feeling me, but I'm not gone just assume that we are together," she admitted. I just looked at her ass because she was acting like she didn't know what was up.

"I thought you knew that you were mine. I didn't think that I had to explain it," I told her ass. I needed her to know what it was with us. She was locked in with me.

"I'm just asking. I don't want to be thinking that you mine and you belong to someone else".

"I mean shit, you done fucking with that nigga, right? So that means that it's my time to shine. I just didn't need to be beefin' with that nigga about you. I chilled and waited for my turn," I admitted.

She just nodded her head. I held her from behind as we watched the camera. I couldn't lie, a nigga wanted to have her ass bent over right there in my office, but I didn't want her to think that was all I wanted. I wanted to really get to know her. There was just something about her vibe.

We ended up chilling in my office until it was time to go. The club closed at three, but we stayed until everything was cleaned up. Once we went our separate ways, I headed to get some pussy because she had a nigga's dick ready to bust. I knew that more than likely, Trinity was up. She worked overnight at the hospital, so she was just getting off. I grabbed my phone from the cup holder and dialed her number.

"Hey baby," she answered.

"What you got going?" I asked as I headed towards her house. I knew that I was going there so there was no use in wasting time.

"Shit, baby. Just got in the house. You finna come by?"

"Yeah, I will be there in a minute," I told her before we

ended the call. The whole ride there, my mind was on Maci. I pulled up at her house in no time. I grabbed my weed, gun, and Backwoods before getting out and heading to the door. When I walked in, she was in the kitchen cooking. I walked up behind her and hugged her from the back. She was wearing a big-ass shirt that had her fat ass hanging out the back. She knew what she was doing. How could a nigga not want to fuck if she was walking around like that? I looked over her shoulder to see that she was cooking. She was making pasta. Trinity was a good girl who could cook, she was just ran through and a nigga couldn't be in a relationship with a bitch that done fucked a million niggas. Niggas that I knew had hit that. She was cool, just not girlfriend material, not for me anyway.

Since was cooking, I went to chill on the couch while she finished. I had chilled all day, so this was just what I needed. I broke my weed down and rolled me a Backwood so that I could enjoy my food. As I said before she was a good cook, so I knew that it was about to be fye.

"Reese, I need help getting my car fixed," she yelled from the kitchen.

"What going on with that junt?" I asked.

"I need some brakes and there is a tire sensor light on," she explained. I just shook my head and pulled some money out of my pocket. I fucked with her, so that little shit was nothing. I peeled off six-hundred dollars and placed it on the table. Besides, she never really asked me for anything. I didn't feel like giving a female something was tricking. I felt that if you were laying up with her why not make sure that she was good? That was simply some real nigga shit.

When as I finished smoking, she handed me my food and I dug in. That shit was good as fuck. She finished before me, so she came back and grabbed my plate. Just as she was walking off, my text went off.

Maci: hey just letting you know I made it in. I'm finna lay down. I gotta go to my other job in a few hours.

Me: ok baby girl call when you get up

She had a nigga smiling at that simple ass text. I was happy to know that she remembered to text me. That showed that she was thinking about me.

"Damn who got you smiling and shit?" Trinity asked, pulling my thoughts from Maci.

"You would be if you were in yo knees sucking my dick," I told her as I relaxed back on the couch. She was worried about the wrong shit. Just like I thought she would, she dropped to the floor and pulled my dick out. That was all that she needed to worry about.

8
MACI

TWO WEEKS LATER

"Girl, you really think he gone fire you?" Kresha asked as she laid across my bed. We were chilling because we both were off the whole weekend. I had been telling her that I wanted to take a vacation. I wanted a chance to just relax. We were always doing shit, so it was nice to just chill.

"Let's go to the mall. I want to get me some shoes," Kresha said as she scrolled through her phone. I just nodded. I was busy looking at Lee's Facebook. He was on it doing the most like I wasn't friends with him. What he didn't know was that he was just making me even more disgusted with him. It was like all the love was gone. I cared about him living, but that was about it. I didn't want him at all. I was over being hurt. I wanted to be happy and that was just what I was going to do.

I had my times when I wanted to go back to him because that was what I was used to, but then I thought about all the shit that he had done. There was no way that I would once again subject myself to the hurt that he had caused me over the years. Just thinking about that shit had me mad. I had let that nigga play me for way too long. I would never let another nigga do me the way that I had let him do me.

I got up so that I could get dressed. I loved when I had off-days. I would be happy when I was in the position to only work one job. I was tired of working so much. I felt like I was missing out so much. I was twenty and living like I was forty. I wanted to go on vacation and travel the world, and I knew that was not going to happen as long as I was working my ass off. Hell, I never had a chance to enjoy the money that I was making. Kresha and I planned to move soon. I knew that was going to be hard because we were so used to being here with her family.

"I'm finna go get dressed," she said as she walked out of my room. I grabbed my clothes and headed to the bathroom. I wanted to go in before her because I knew that she was going to take all day. Once I was done, I went back to my room so that I could curl my hair. After about three hours, we were getting ready to walk out the door.

"We need to go and look at that apartment, cause girl I'm so ready," I cooed as we got in the car.

"Shit, me too girl. I love mama and them, but I want my own space. Hell, living with they asses, my ass will be single forever. Ma ass too nosey. She be all in my business," Kresha said as she started the car. I was happy that she was driving. I hated driving.

"That ain't got shit to do with Ma. Yo' ass gotta give somebody a chance first," I joked. She went through some shit with her ex, but I don't talk about it because that's her story to tell.

Reese: wyd

Me: on the way to the mall

Reese: bet

I didn't reply because I knew that meant that he was going to meet me there. Maybe he would have his brother so that he and Kresha could see each other again. I loved to see them together. I had no idea why she didn't want to talk to him. He was fine and paid. I could tell that she liked him, but I guess her past was keeping her from giving him a real chance.

For the rest of the ride, we talked about all kinds of shit. Star ended up calling and telling us that she was going to meet us at the mall. I was happy that we were all back. I missed her crazy ass. She was the life of the party. When we pulled to the mall, we found a parking space and headed to meet with her since she beat us there. When we walked into the mall, she was standing to the side on her phone.

"What's up bitches," she smiled as she greeted us with the phone still to her face. I knew that she was on the phone with her dude as always. I was so happy that she had found someone to love her the way that she needed to be loved. I wished that I had that type of love.

"Girl, you so ghetto," Kresha joked as she hugged her. Just as they hugged, my phone went off.

Reese: WYA

Me: By Sephora

"Let's go in here. I need some finishing spray," Star said as she walked into the store. We followed behind. I hated coming in here because I was always buying some shit that I didn't need. I walked around picking up shit until I saw both Reese and Jim walk into the store. Just like every other bitch in the store, my focus went to them. Reese walked over to me and hugged me from the back as he always did anytime that he was around me. I was not used to the type of affection that he showed me. Lee never did stuff like that.

"Hey baby," he greeted me before kissing me on my neck. I had fussed a million times about him doing that. I told him to stop doing it but of course, he didn't listen. I just smiled. Any time that he was close to me, I got butterflies.

"Why she be giving my boy such a hard time?" he laughed as he watched Jim dote all over Kresha. I didn't know why she was playing hard to get. Star was still shopping, so we all walked around until her slow ass was ready to check out.

Once we all checked out, we headed to Gucci. Star's man was already shopping when we walked in. I took a seat. I would have loved to be able to buy this high price shit, but that would have to wait till a later time.

"Why are you sitting over here?" Reese asked as he pulled me to my feet. I couldn't lie, this nigga had me open. I loved the way that he was always all over me. I was always the focus of his attention.

"No reason," I lied. I walked behind him as he looked at shit. They had some nice ass bags.

"This that bag that you were looking at online," Kresha said as she held up a bag. I grabbed it and looked it over. It looked better than I thought that it would.

"Girl it looks better than I thought it would. I'm going to get next month," I told her. Reese grabbed it from me and walked off. Both Kresha and I shrugged and walked to the show section. I couldn't wait until my ass was able to afford shit like this.

"Hey, would you like to try those on?" the sales associate asked.

"Yea, she wants to try them. Tell her what size you need," Reese said as he walked back over to us. I stared at him. He knew that I didn't want him buying me shit. That wasn't why I was with him.

"Give her yo' size, too. I like these as well," Jim said to Kresha. I knew that she was going to turn him down.

"I wear a 39," she said, shocking me.

"I need a 38," I added before she walked off. Kresha was looking unbothered, and that made me wonder what they were talking about before I walked up. They both walked off, leaving me and Reese alone again. It was like any time that we were alone, my heart was beating out of my chest. I had no idea what he was doing to me.

I mean even when we talked on the phone, I would get butterflies. He was everything that a woman would want. He was so consistent. Total opposite of Lee's ass.

"Why are you looking like that?" He asked as we browsed the store.

"Nothing, this just new to me. I told you that. My ex never really bought me anything, especially nothing this expensive," I admitted. Lee bought me shit, but nothing like this.

"Baby this just the beginning. This small shit. I told you to open up and let me show you what it's like to be with a real man, baby. I can give you the world, you just have to let me," he said as he kissed me on the neck making chills course through my body. I just nodded my head. We ended up going to a few other stores before we headed to get something to eat.

Star and Lo had something to do, so they went their own way. We ended up going to Ruth Chris. I had only been there once and that was for Kresha's eighteenth birthday. We ended up sitting at different tables because Reese said that he wanted to talk with me. I was so shocked that Kresha was cool with that. They sat directly across from us.

"So, you gone let a nigga love you?" he asked me, pulling my focus from the menu. I just looked at him because I really didn't know how to answer him. I had just gotten out of a relationship, so I didn't know if I wanted to jump right back in one. At the same time, I didn't want to miss out on him.

"Reese, I just can't take being hurt again. So, if you know that you still wanna be in the streets, then let's just leave shit how it been," I explained. He was sitting across from me, but for the life of me, I couldn't look at him. It was like he made me nervous or some shit.

"Maci, look at me. You are a queen baby and I want to treat you as such."

I was lost for words. It was like he was saying all the right things. I just didn't know if I wanted to believe him. I knew that Reese had a million hoes. I had known him for a while, so I knew all about him in the streets. I had seen females fight over this nigga, so I knew what was up with him. I didn't want the drama that I knew that he would bring.

"Why you so quiet?" he asked me. I looked up from the menu that I was feigning interest in. I just didn't want to look at him. Maci made me realize that I was lonely as fuck. I hadn't been with anyone since my ex, and I couldn't lie a bitch needed to get fucked. My Rose vibrator wasn't doing shit for me now. I needed some pressure ASAP. I wanted to get fucked good. Fuck, that I need that shit.

"I'm just trying to see what I want to eat," I lied. I was really trying to avoid his gaze. I swear he was so sexy.

"Mane, that's bullshit. You been looking at that motherfucker since we walked in here. That motherfucker not that big," he laughed. I didn't know what to say. "So, you just gone look at me like I'm crazy?"

"Naw" I laughed. "I just don't like looking in your face, it gives me thoughts that I shouldn't be having. So to keep that from happening I'm looking at the menu," I said bluntly.

I had a feeling that he was going to give me issues and that was something that I didn't want. My life was peaceful. Star told me that he had two baby mamas and that was some drama that I didn't need. What I did need was for him to knock this pussy out of the park.

"Tell me what's on yo' mind baby girl," he said as he licked his lips. That shit had me wondering if he ate pussy well. He had been in jail, so he may have forgotten how to do it. Or shit, as fine as he was, I'm sure he was fucking a guard.

'*I'm thinking about how them juicy ass lips would feel on this pussy,*' I thought to myself.

"Nothing," I lied. There was no way that I was going to tell him what I was really thinking. The girl came and took our order which saved me from talking to his ass. Just as she came back with our drinks, my phone rang. I looked down and it was a number that I didn't know, so I hit ignore because I didn't want to be rude. I sat my phone down and it rang again. I ignored once again. Just as I was about to power it off, a text came through.

901666-3344: bet

I had no idea who it was and didn't care. I was trying to enjoy dinner with this fine-ass man. I didn't want any distractions at all. I wanted him to have all my attention. We talked about random shit until our food came out. The whole time that I was eating he was watching me. Now it was my turn to ask questions.

"What's on yo' mind while you over there looking at me like that?" I asked. Although I wasn't sure if I wanted to know the answer. I could tell by the way that he was looking that he was going to say something nasty.

"I'm thinking about what I'm going to do when I get a hold of yo fine ass," he admitted. I smiled because we were thinking the same thing. I wanted his ass in the worst way.

"Show me," I said before I had a chance to stop myself.

"Say no mo'," he said while getting up pulling out a wad of money. He placed two-hundred-dollar bills on the table before sticking his hand out to help me up. I wanted my steak, but I wanted his ass more.

"We finna roll. Ima hit you up later bro," was all he said before damn near dragging me off towards the door. I was anxious as hell.

Mai: what the hell was that about.

Me: Girllll I will tell you later

I knew that she was going to have a million questions, but I didn't care. I was done letting my past dictate what I did or who I dealt with. As of today, I was living for me. I wanted to live life on the edge. Hell, my ass was on edge thinking about what was about to happen. I just hoped the nigga had some good dick because I would hate to look at him differently.

He held my hand the entire car ride. I was on my phone, but I could feel him taking glances at me. Shit, my ass was doing the same thing.

I was in awe as we pulled up to his house. He must have had a lot of money to be able to afford this getting right out of jail. Honestly, I didn't care because I didn't need his money. I had my own, so I was good. I just needed his dick. He helped me out of the car, and I followed him to the door. When I walked in the door, I pushed his ass to the wall. There was no need for us to talk.

"Damn," was all that he was able to get out. I kissed his soft lips. That alone had me dripping. After he got over the shock of me attacking him, he attacked me, and baby I let that nigga have his way. He picked me up and carried me to the couch.

I felt like a kid as I anticipated what he was going to do to me. As soon as he laid me down, he pulled my jeans down. It was like I was in high school, and this was my first-time having sex.

"Can I have my way?" he asked as he helped me out of my shirt. Once I was undressed, he stood back and looked at me. It was as if he was trying to see what he wanted to do next. I needed my head and he pulled me to the end of the couch. "I need to hear you say that I can have my way."

"Yes, you can have your way with me, baby," I told him as he dropped to his knees. The moment that his tongue touched my clit, I felt like I wanted to jump out of my skin. His touch was so soft. The way that he kissed my pussy sent chills through my body. He was so gentle with me and that was new. My ex was always rough, and he never ate my pussy.

Jim was the fucking *business*. That nigga took his time with my body, and I was all for that. By the time that we were done fucking, all I could think about was the next time that I was going to get handled by his fine ass.

I laid back in his big ass bed and thought about that Tik Tok where the girl goes over the dude's house for the first time. *"This bitch pressure this fucking bed pressure here...and the Wi-Fi jumping in this bitch. Im finna start comin g over here. "* I,burst into laughing at the thought, causing him to look over at me.

"What's funny?" he asked sitting his phone down.

"Nothing, I was thinking about this Tik Tok," I admitted.

"What the fuck is a Tik Tok?" he asked, causing me to laugh again. I had forgotten that his ass had been in jail, so he really didn't know about all of that. I grabbed my phone and unlocked it before going to the Tik Tok app. I had the video saved, so I was able to go straight to it. I played the video and watch his facial expressions. Lord this man was fine as hell. I knew I had thought that to myself a million times, but shit, I couldn't help it.

After watching, he took my phone and started scrolling. I laid back and watched him. As soon as I laid back, he grabbed me and pulled me closer. I just smiled and laid my head on his chest. It was like this was where I belonged. He made me feel secure something that I had felt in a long time.

"This shit funny as hell," he said as he continued to watch videos. I was dozing off until he kissed my forehead. I looked in his eyes, and that shit sent chills through my body.

"Why you single Kresha?" he questioned. I didn't know if I needed to be truthful or not. I didn't want to run him away. I knew that the truth would do that for sure.

"I just need time to get me together. I had goals that I wanted to meet, and I knew that a man would distract me from that," I halfway confessed. That was part of the reason, so technically I didn't lie. I just didn't tell the whole truth. I had a past that I was not proud of, and I didn't want him to know that side of me.

◎❧◎

A WEEK LATER

It had been five days since I had heard from Jim. I was in my room listening to music scrolling on Facebook. It was the only thing that I could do to keep from thinking about his ass. It was like no matter how much I tried, my mind wouldn't focus on anything but him. I did not understand why it was that way considering we had just met. There was just something about his vibe that had me stuck. I had been calling him, but he wasn't answering. He would reply to a text here and there, but that was all that I could get out of him.

I was over it. I was not about to be losing sleep over a nigga that I had just met. He had me deep in my feelings and that was not me. I had been single for damn near two years. I talked to a few niggas here and there, but no one ever gave off the vibe that he did.

The first day that we chilled, it felt like we had known each other forever. That shit felt like love-at-first sight to be honest. I hated to say it, but I knew that I loved that nigga the second he kissed me. I could go on and on about the things that I loved about him. God had made this man perfectly. I wasn't sure what made me fall, but I had fallen hard.

I felt like a fool. I had previously been in love with a nigga who tried to take my life. I had to shake that shit because if I didn't, I would end up showing that nigga a side of me that he didn't even know existed. It was crazy because I didn't know this nigga, but he had a bitch ready to act a fool.

"Bitch you in here with this shit all loud like you going through a heartbreak or some shit," Maci said as she walked into my room. We had moved into our apartment a few days ago, so I was able to play the music as loud as I wanted. When I was at home with my mother, I was never able to do that.

"Bitch shut up. You working tonight?" I asked, changing the subject. I didn't want to talk about what I was going through or how I was feeling about Jim. That was another story for another day. I would tell her when the time was right.

"Girl, yes. Hopefully, he does not fire my ass tonight. He has been doing the most," she rolled her eyes. I couldn't do shit but laugh because he had been telling her that he was going to fire her since they started messing around. I knew that she was going to be mad because that job brought in the most money.

"You need to go up there. I talked to Star, she said that she was coming through," she advised. I gave a blank stare. I didn't really want to go. After all, I knew that I would run into him since he was part owner. Just as I was about to reply, my phone rang and I saw that it was Star.

"Yall bitches think y'all slick," I answered the Facetime call. They both just laughed.

"So, you going hoe?" Star asked. I knew that I could not tell them both no, so I just went on and agreed. I had no idea what I wanted to wear. I really didn't want to get all dressed up.

"Yeah, damn," I said hanging up on Star. I can lie I wanted to see him, but then I didn't. Maybe I didn't want to potentially see him with another female. This nigga had me dickmatized. I knew that I could have called or texted, but I wanted him to reach out. I wanted to know that I was on his mind like he was on mine.

I looked at the time and saw that it was almost seven, so I knew I needed to get my life together. I needed to make sure that I was looking good. I walked into my huge closet and looked around. I was so happy that we had a place of our own. It was a nice two-bedroom downtown. From my window, I had a view of the river, and Maci had a view of the bridge. I would never have thought that we would be living somewhere like this. We had been saving up for almost a year. We wanted to get a house, but this was a much better option for us since we both worked so much.

I thumbed through my clothes to see what I wanted to throw on. I wanted to be comfortable. So, I decided that I would just wear jeans and a crop top with some heels. I had been waiting to wear the Gucci heels that he bought me.

My hair was in its natural state because I had washed it the night before, so I plugged my flat iron in so that I could do something to it. I changed my music to get myself in the partying mood. It had been so long since we went out, I was more than ready. Hell, if he didn't act right, maybe I could find a nigga to fuck me as good as he did. I laughed at myself knowing that he was the only dick that I wanted in me.

"Bitch, I hope you ready," Maci yelled as she walked into my room. I had just straightened the last piece of hair as she walked in. Her ass already had her hair done so she didn't have shit to do. I smirked at her. She knew damn well that I was not ready, it had only been a few hours. She rolled her eyes and walked out of the room. Once I put my flat irons up, I got started on my makeup. By the time that I was almost done, my phone was ringing. I figured that it was Star, so I answered with my air pods since the phone was on the other side of the room.

"Hello," I answered.

"Damn so you haven't seen me calling you?" my ex, Nell, asked. I should have looked before answering.

"What do you want Nell?" I asked as I continued to finish my makeup.

"Damn, I can't call you?"

"I'm just trying to see what would make you call me?" I asked as I cleaned up my mess. Nell knew damn well that I didn't want to talk to him. I was done with him and anything that was connected to his ass. Nell was who I thought that I was going to spend my life with, but now I never wanted to see him again. The fact that he was calling let me know that he did not understand that.

"So, who is the nigga that you been out there with?" he asked as if it was any of his business. Niggas like him killed the. He wanted to break me down but there was no way that I was going to let that happen.

"Nell, is that why you called? Because if it is then you wasted your time. It doesn't matter would I'm with. Just know that I'm not with you," I said before ending the call. There was nothing else for us to talk about. I was not about to let him get in my head. I was past that phase in life.

I slipped my clothes on before heading to see what Maci was doing. When I walked into her room, she was on Facetime with Reese as always.

"Damn, y'all finna see each other," I said interrupting their conversation.

"Girl don't worry about us," she said before turning around and saying, "Okay boo, you look good as fuck. Jim gone be all over yo' ass." I rolled my eyes because she was doing the most while she was on the phone with Reese. I didn't need him thinking that I was coming for Jim's ass. I was going because I wanted to have fun.

After she ended her call, Star and Lo pulled up. I hated that they were always on some double dating shit. At the same time, I was happy for both of them. Love is a beautiful thing, and I would be happy when I found it.

We laughed and joked the entire way to the club. "Maci, I thought you were working?" I asked.

"I was, but he told me that I could chill tonight, so I'm chilling," she informed me. She was blushing like a schoolgirl. As we pulled up, Jim and Reese were walking out the door. As soon as the car came to a stop, Jim opened the door for me. He reached his hand out to help me out of the car. It was as if no one else was there.

"What's up beautiful," he said, pulling me in for a hug. My pussy was wet as fuck just from that. There was just something about this man that was driving my ass crazy.

"Aw, you remember me," I said as I pulled away from him. I knew that I was going to have to go straight to the bathroom when I got in the club so that I could clean myself up. I was so into his ass that I didn't notice that everyone else was gone on the club.

"Baby I can never forget you. A nigga just been busy," he said as he led me into the club. I wanted to say something else, but there was no need because he was not my man so there was no need to question him or make a big deal about it. It was what it was, so I was good. This nigga held my hand all the way to the VIP. I couldn't lie, a bitch felt good. His ass was all over me, and I was all for it. I knew that I should have been mad that he ghosted me but all that went out the window the moment that I laid eye on his fine ass.

9

JIM

A FEW DAYS LATER

"Baby, we need to go and get Lil Jim some shoes," Kayla called out from the bathroom. I had been over there with them and me and Kayla was working on us. It felt good being with my son and her. That lil' nigga was just like me. Being around Kayla was cool too. She made sure a nigga was straight. She cooked and all that. I stayed over there because I didn't want her to think that she could come to my shit whenever she wanted to. I fucked with her, but Kresha had put a stain on a nigga brain. I had been thinking about her ass non-stop. I knew that she thought that I had forgotten about her, but I hadn't. just had a lot of shit going on.

"Okay, I will give you the money. I got some shit to do today," I told her as I finished getting dressed.

"Okay, baby," she said as she looked through her drawers. I was happy that she didn't make a big deal like she did everything else. That was why I didn't want to get into this shit with her. I knew that she was going to start that shit. She knew that I nigga was in the streets, yet she wanted me with her every night. Shit, if I laid up with her ass all day, I couldn't make no money. I wanted to be done with this street shit, so I was grinding.

I finished getting dressed and then headed to see what my son was doing. When I walked in his room, he was on the floor playing his game.

"Hey daddy." He greeted me as soon as he noticed that I was in his room.

"What's good, son? You chillin' at home or you wanna go to your granny house?" I asked, taking a seat on his bed. I knew that he loved to go to my mama's house because he knew that Jamiya was always there. I loved the bond that my kids had. They loved being around each other. As a father, I was going to make sure that it stayed that way.

"Yea, I wanna play the game with Miya. We made a bet on 2k. We are betting on our allowance," he admitted. I just shook my head. My kids were crazy.

"Get up and get dressed so we can roll," I told him before heading back to the room. When I walked in, Kayla was in the bathroom on the phone. I couldn't tell who she was talking to, but I knew that she was going back and forth with someone.

"That don't matter. That's his daddy so he gone be here because that's where his son is," she spoke. It got quiet, so I knew that whoever she was talking to was speaking.

"Okay, I will call when he leaves Co," she said before I heard her flush the toilet. I walked out the room. . She had told me that she was talking to a nigga while I was gone, but she said that they stopped fucking off before I came home. The fact she was explaining herself to the nigga meant that they were still fucking off.

I helped my son get dressed and we headed out the door. I didn't say shit to her ass. I was good on her. I knew how niggas worked and I was not about to be beefing with a nigga over a female, especially one that was not really mine. She had to really care about the nigga to be going back and forth with him.

The whole ride all I could think about was the fact that she tried me. That shit had a nigga pissed. She knew me and how I got down, so why would she be on some shit like that? She had me looking at her like she was the opps. I didn't care that she was talking to a nigga it was just that nigga. He was from the other side so she should respect that shit.

I dropped my son off and headed to the hood. Since I had been home, I had shown my face but not much. I wanted to see what was going on at my traps. I mean Lo had them laced with cameras, but there was nothing like being there. I stopped at the store and got my something to drink and some backwoods before heading there. When I pulled up, the block was jumping. I couldn't deny that I missed this shit. I parked in the driveway and jumped out.

This was the first house that me and my brother had gotten. It was right across from the projects. I remembered when we used to rent this house from my grandmothers' friend. When her husband died, she sold it to us because she didn't want to keep up with it. That was the first investment that we made.

"What's good boss man," a young nigga named Lou spoke as I walked up. I liked the lil nigga. He was a born hustla. I made a mental note to ask my brother about him. With the right guidance, he could be something.

"What's good, come in the house and holla at me," I told him as I walked past. I was happy that my brother made sure that they kept it clean. I did not want this shit to look like a trap. I like to be in a clean environment. I took a seat on the couch, and he sat on the chair.

"So, tell me your goals," I asked. I wanted to see where his head was at. I wanted to know what he wanted out of this shit.

"I'm hustling to make sure my daughter has everything she needs. I cut hair as well, so I want to open a few shops in the city. I wanna make it out this shit alive and free. I also want to get my granny out the hood," he spoke. I just nodded as I thought about what he was saying. I liked the fact that he wanted to get out of this shit one day. Most niggas liked this fast money, so they had no goals other than to be rich.

"How old are you?"

"Eighteen," he admitted.

"I see potential in you, so I want to see you make out of this shit. You remind me of a younger me," I admitted. He smiled just as my brother and Lo walked in the door. We talked a while longer, then I let him get back to the money.

Once he was outside, I told my brother what I had in mind for him. Reese agreed with my logic. I wanted to back up and let someone else handle the street shit. We all decided to go outside and chill. It had been so long since I had done that. Since I had been home, I had been moving nonstop. It was nice to have a moment to just chill. My life was so busy with the club, apartments and street shit.

"Star said they finna pull up," Lo informed us. I just smiled thinking about Kresha and that good ass pussy she had. I couldn't lie, a nigga had been thinking about her ass nonstop. We texted a few times, but that was about it. She had me feeling like I was the female, and she was the nigga.

"Good cause I need to holla at her friend. She around here treating a nigga like I'm fuck-boy, be half texting a nigga back and shit," I admitted. They all laughed, but I didn't find shit funny. I was dead serious. She had me fucked up, that was going to be my pussy fa sho'. Especially now that I knew that Kayla was on some other shit. I rolled a Backwood while we watched the kids play and shit.

"Here this bitch go," Lou said as a car pull in front of the house. He dropped his head, so I knew that it was about to be some shit.

"Lou, so you don't see me calling your phone?" she said soon as she jumped out.

"Come on with that bull shit Mena," Lou said without

moving. I could tell that she had done this before because he seemed unbothered by it. She was fine as hell, but the way that she was acting was not cute at all.

"I knew you been laid up with yo' hoe ass baby mama," she yelled. I wanted to see how he was going to handle this. That would tell me a lot about his character. He sighed, grabbed her and walked her in the house.

"I don't miss that shit at all," Lo said just as Star's Benz pulled up. I was happy for my nigga because he deserved that shit, especially after what he had gone through with his ex. Star was good for his nerdy ass. Lo was a silent killer. If you looked at his ass, you would think that he was a geek. Now don't get me wrong, he was smart as hell, but he could kill a motherfucker with his bare hands. His mama and my mama were best friends before she passed. My mama took him in as her own and we had been rocking since. He was my brother and there was no one that could tell me different.

The girls got out the car. Star walked on the porch and so did Maci. Kresha just stood next to it. She had her head down in her phone, but I knew that she could feel me looking at her. I got up just as Lou and his girl came out the house. She was all smiles and giggles. That's the way that shit should have been. I liked how he handled that shit like a real man. I hated public drama. You could act any way that you wanted at home, but around people was another story. He sat in the seat that I was in, and she sat on his lap. I then focused my attention on Kresha.

"Why you all the way over there?" I asked as I approached her.

"What I'm coming up there for?" she asked. I knew that she was in her feelings because a nigga had been distant, but that was going to change. I was just trying to half-ass do right because a nigga didn't want to hurt her.

"So, you don't want to be around a nigga?" I questioned. She just looked at me. I knew that she wanted to say something, but there were a lot of people around. I respected that shit. I grabbed her hand and pulled her towards the house. As soon as I closed the door, I kissed her soft ass lips. I could do that shit all day.

"Why you be doing that? Jim, you make time for the shit that you want to make time for. I just respect and understand that I'm just not one of those things," she expressed. That shit had a nigga feeling bad because I didn't want her to feel that way. I liked her I just had a lot going on. I stood back and looked at her. She was dressed so simply, but looked so good. Let not talk about how good she smelled.

"I promise I'm going to do better, sexy," I kissed her again. This time she kissed me back. It was on from that point. I took her back to the back because I didn't want anyone to walk in on us. They knew what we were doing, but I still wasn't taking any chances.

The door closed and undressed. I loved that shit. It meant that she was ready for a nigga. I watched as she laid back on the bed with her legs wide open. Kresha was a different kind of woman when she was in the bedroom. She was the definition of "a lady in the streets and freak in the sheets". Nothing was off limits when we were in the bed.

"Come fuck me," she demanded. I wasted no time diving in that pussy. I wanted to taste her, but we didn't have much time. There was no telling what could pop off. As soon as I was in, I closed my eyes. I had to compose myself because her shit was so wet that a nigga would bust right then.

"Fuck baby," I moaned out as she moved her hips. This girl's pussy was so fucking good. I could fuck her for the rest of my life.

10
KAYLA

"Bitch why the fuck yo baby daddy in the hood with some other bitch?!" my cousin Brittany yelled in the phone soon as I answered. I had to pull the phone from my face to be sure that I was hearing her correctly. I knew that Jim wasn't playing with me like that. He knew that I didn't play that. I told him that I was not going to let him play with me like that again. I had something for his ass as soon as he got home tonight. I had some other shit to do right now.

"Girl, who is the bitch?" I asked.

"I don't know her. I was at KeKe house, and I saw them go in the house together. She was with the Star bitch," she finished. Star was a bitch that I could not stand. We used to be cool, but she got with her nigga and started acting funny. You know how bitches be, they get money and switch up.

"I'm finna call you back." I hung the phone up and dialed Jim because I wanted to see if he was going to answer. I wasn't going to ask him about it until he got home. I called his phone and didn't get an answer. I waited a few minutes to see if he would call back, but he didn't. It was cool because I was going to see for myself. I knew that he wasn't with the drama, so I wasn't going to say anything I just wanted to see. I told him that I was a different person now, and he was about to see that.

Just as I was about to walk out the house, my phone rang I damn near dropped everything in my hand trying to get it out my purse. I was disappointed as hell when I saw that it was Co calling.

"What's up?" I answered.

"Where you at?" he asked. I hated to be rushed. I told him that I was coming so why was he calling me? Co had been a little over-bearing since he found out that Jim was home. It was like he always wanted to be around me. I loved Co, I just loved my baby daddy more. I knew at some point I was going to have to let one of them go.

"Baby, I'm on the way," I assured him. I had been spending as much time as I could with Co while Jim's ass was in the streets. I knew that soon I was going to have to stop because Jim was going to notice with his nosey ass. I knew my baby daddy, he paid attention to everything.

"Ok baby I'm waiting. A nigga misses you," he told me, causing me to blush. I missed his crazy ass too. Co and Jim were alike in many ways, but they were different at the same time. There were things that I could say and do around Co and he wouldn't say a word, but if I tried that same shit around Jim, my ass would be dead. Jim's ass didn't play, that's why I was treading lightly around him.

"I will call you when I'm outside," I told him before ending the call. Once I was in the car settled, I called Jim's ass again. He didn't answer this time either. I didn't want to believe her because I knew that he would never come home and do me like that, but he was making me think otherwise. If he played with me, I was going to show him who I was. I was not giving him a chance to play with me again.

The whole way to Co's house, I was thinking about Jim. I was in love. My baby daddy was that nigga, but shit, so was Co. They were from two different areas, so they carried themselves two different ways as I said before. It didn't take me long to get to Co's house. When I pulled up, I texted and told him that I was outside. I waited for him to come to the door before I got out the car. I loved his house. It was so nice. He was dressed in nothing but some basketball shorts and socks. He was smelling good. When he hugged me, I laid my head on his chest.

"Damn, you looking good baby," he told me as I walked past him. I sat my purse down and went straight to the kitchen. He wanted me to cook him something to eat. I washed my hands and got right to it. I was making baked chicken with wild rice and asparagus. Something quick because I didn't know when Jim's ass would be calling.

"So, you and the nigga back together?" Co asked, catching me off guard.

"Where at come from?"

"I just asked a question Kay." I knew then that he was pissed because that was the only time that he didn't call me baby. I hadn't told him about Jim living at my house. Anytime that he had tried to come over, I would just tell him that Lil Jim was home. We already had an understanding that he couldn't come over if my baby was home. Jim's ass would kill me if I had another nigga around our son. Plus, I knew that lil Jim would tell his daddy, and I didn't have time for that drama.

"I mean he home, but I'm with you," I lied. He walked up behind me and hugged me. When he kissed my neck, I exhaled air that I didn't know that I was holding. His kisses were so soft. That shit had me wet, but I needed to finish cooking.

"Good. I want you here with me tonight. A nigga had a long week. I just wanna lay with my baby and have some peace," he added. I knew that if I told him that I couldn't that he would be mad, so I had to decide who I wanted to be mad at me.

"Okay baby," I lied. I was going to just wait till later and tell him that I had to go and get my baby. I knew there was no way that Jim would let me get away with not coming home, even if my son wasn't home. He walked off and since I was waiting on the oven to heat up, I headed to get my phone.

Me: bitch why he just say that he wants me to spend the night

Brit: so, what you gone do bitch

Me: I don't know. You know Jim's ass will have a fit if I don't come home.

Brit: girl please that nigga with another bitch he not thinking about yo ass right now

Brit: tell him you fell asleep at my house

Me: ok

I didn't think that was going to work, but I was damn sure going to try because I didn't want to lose Co just yet. I kicked my shoes off and headed to go and finish cooking. The whole time that I was cooking, I was thinking of what I was going to tell Jim. Or hell, *if* I was going to tell him anything at all. He was with another bitch anyway, so why did I care about how his ass felt? Let me stop bullshitting, of course I cared. I didn't know if what she said was true because she was known to lie. If she saw him near Ke Ke's house, then that meant that he was at the trap, so the female could have been buying something from him. I just didn't want to jump to conclusions.

Me: hey baby wyd

Baby Daddy: shit at the spot

Me: aw ok I was just checking on you I called but you didn't answer

After I sent that text, I held the phone waiting on a reply. I knew that if he was working that he may have not seen it. I made a mental note to turn his read receipts on. I wanted to know when he read my shit. I didn't know why I hadn't thought of that before now. I needed to know his moves, so I decided to turn on his location as well. That meant I could move the way that I wanted to. If I could watch his moves, then I could really keep this shit going with Co.

I ended up finishing dinner faster than I thought. Once I was done, I sat the table and went to find Co. I walked in his man cave where he was playing the game. I just stood there and watched his fine ass.

"Baby, dinner ready," I called out from the door. He hated for me to come in his man cave.

"Ok," he said as I walked away.

Baby Daddy: I was busy. where you at

Me: Brit house

Baby Daddy: ok

I didn't worry with replying, I just headed to the table so that I could eat. I didn't need his ass asking any more questions. I stood at the table waiting on Co ass. He always took his time then complained when his food was cold. I even tried fixing his plate when he got to the table and his ass got mad. Just as I was about to go and call for him again, he walked in the dining room. He was so busy texting he damn near walked into me.

"My bad baby," he said, kissing me before sitting down. I took my seat next to him and said grace so that we could eat. The whole time that we were eating, he was in his phone. That shit pissed me off because I wanted all of his attention.

"So, you gone be on yo phone the whole time that I'm here?" I asked with an attitude.

"Naw," was all he said before stuffing his mouth. I rolled my eyes knowing that he was going to pick the phone up again.

"So, what you and that nigga got going on? And don't lie to me." I really didn't know how to answer that because there was no way I was telling him the truth. I just looked at him. Him saying "don't lie to me" let me know that he already had an idea of what was going on.

"Co, that's my baby daddy and that's it. What you done heard because he been home for weeks and all of a sudden you asking me about him?" I questioned.

Co knew how I felt about talking about my baby daddy. He knew that I was not about to discuss Jim with him so there was in use in him asking me anything about him. I knew what he was on, so there was no way that I was going to set him up. I knew Co way better than he thought I did. He could not fool me.

    I cleaned the table and washed dishes before I headed to lay down with him. I planned to lie so that I could leave in the middle of the night. I jumped in the shower and got in the bed. I wasn't in the bed five minutes before the nigga was all over me. I smiled thinking about how good he was about to eat my pussy. I just prayed that he was done asking about Jim.

11

REESE

"Baby, you ready?" I called out to Maci's slow ass. We were headed to look at a building that I was thinking about buying. I loved the fact that she wanted to see a nigga win. I'll be honest, a nigga was lazy, but she didn't let me be that way. She was the first female that I fucked with that really cared about a nigga's well-being. I was falling in love. I hadn't felt real feelings for anyone since my ex, Lexi. I thought that she was the one for me. That was until I found out that she was pregnant by another nigga. That shit fucked my trust up with females. Maci was changing that shit. She was slowly breaking the wall that I had around my heart.

"Come on," she said as she walked in my living room. Since the day that she pulled to the trap we had been stuck to each other. Either I was at her house, or she was at mine, but we had slept together every night. Waking up to her was the shit. She made sure a nigga ate every day. I couldn't see how a nigga could fuck over a woman like her.

I let her walk out the door so that I could lock it behind us. Plus, I loved to watch her from behind. My baby was thick as hell. Today she was dressed in jeans and a fitted shirt with heels. That shit was so sexy. One day she would be rocking J's and heels the next. Once I made sure that she was in the car, I got in and we headed to get shit done. I had planned to fire her at the club and hire her as my assistant because she was good at handling business. I wanted to talk to my brother first because she would be doing it for the both of us. Just as I was pulling out the gate, I saw a car that looked like Trinity's car. The car turned the corner so fast that I really didn't get a good look at it.

"So, what we eating today?" she asked as I merged on the expressway. The building that we were going to look at was for a restaurant that I wanted to open. Jim wanted to make a bar and grill, but I wanted some upscale shit.

"Whatever you want baby. Its yo' world I'm just living in it," I told her. She knew that, so I didn't know why she asked.

"Okay, I want rice," she said. When we pulled up to the building, my brother was already there, as always. He was the most punctual person that I knew, and he hated for other people to be late.

We got out the car, and as soon as he saw Maci he laughed. He swore that I was in love. I didn't feel like I was but in his eyes, I was. Just like he swore that he didn't love Kresha's ass, but I knew better. He was with her ass anytime that she wasn't at work. I knew that sooner or later the drama was coming because he and I both knew that Kayla was not going to let his ass go. I told him when he came home that he shouldn't have gotten involved with her like that. I knew that she was fucking with the opps, I just didn't want to ruin his outlook on his precious Kayla. In her defense, she may not have known that he was the opps, but how could she not when he was from the other side?

"This place is huge," Maci said as she walked around. She was actually the one that had found the place for us. I told her that she needed to look into real estate. We stood back and let her do the talking, and by the time that she was done they had gone down on the price of the building. Once everything was settled, we headed out. Jim said that he was going to get the kids, so me and Maci headed to eat. The whole way there she talked about how happy she was that I allowed her to handle that deal for us.

I made a mental note to do something nice for her to show my appreciation. When we pulled up to the valet, I jumped out because I didn't want him opening the door for my woman. I didn't like that shit at all. I held my hand out to help her out the car. My baby was so fucking beautiful. She was all that a nigga wanted.

Just as we walked in the restaurant, I wanted to turn around, but it was too late. Trinity had already spotted me. I just prayed that she didn't make a scene. I knew that she was full of drama, so I knew that she was going to make shit harder than it had to be. My baby was in her phone, so she didn't see that Trinity was staring us down. The hostess showed us to our table, and I was elated that it was in the back. Once we were seated, we started looking over the menu. Just as the waiter walked up, Trinity hit the corner. I dropped my head knowing shit was going to go left. Maci's ass had no chill.

"Hey Reese," Trinity said, making Maci look up from the menu. Her eyes darted from me to Trinity. I couldn't lie, I didn't know if I needed to speak or not. I just looked at her ass. I hadn't been in a relationship in so long, so this shit was new. I didn't have anyone that I had to report to, so a female speaking to me had never been a problem. I would have thought that Trinity would have gotten the picture by now. I hadn't been answering her, but that didn't stop her from calling me at least once a day. It had gotten so bad that she would call from different numbers. I couldn't tell you how many numbers that I had blocked.

After Maci didn't say anything, I took that as my cue to send her about her way. "Trinity, don't you see I'm with my woman?" I asked firmly. I wanted today to be a good day.

"I just wanted to know why you not answering me," she stupidly said. I stared in disbelief. There was no way that she was this damn slow. Trinity was an educated woman.

"Aye, didn't he just tell you that he was with his woman? There is no way that you that slow. We trying to eat, so can you go about yo' business," Maci said without looking up from the menu.

"I wasn't talking to you," trinity blurted. I knew then that shit was about to go left because Maci sat the menu down. She scooted the chair back, causing me to perk up. Trinity was doing too much.

I nudged Trinity away because I knew that Maci was going to knock her ass out and I didn't want that to happen. There was no way that I was going to let her go to jail for this bitch. I looked towards the door and saw that security was coming. Good. I didn't need this attention.

"I didn't *ask* you who you was talking to. If you talking to him then you talking to me. That's all me. So, I would advise you to move around. You rude as fuck, who fucking raised you?" Maci said as she grabbed her purse. We left Trinity's ass right there talking to security. I knew that this was not going to be the last time that this happened. Trinity was obsessed with me. I prayed that I didn't have to kill her ass.

When we got in the car Maci popped her air pods in her ears. That meant that she didn't want me talking to her. I headed towards her house. I wanted to ask her if she wanted to go somewhere else, but I didn't want to argue. I pulled up to her house. She got out the car without saying a word to me. I wanted to run behind her, but I wanted to give her some time. When she closed the door, I called my brother.

"Yo," he answered.

"Meet me at Maggie's," I told him. Maggie's was a bar that was owned by my grandfather. My mother ran it now since my father was no longer here. Any time that I was in a bad mood, I went there. It made me feel like I was close to my father. This was his favorite place to be. It seemed like he was in the building. Sometimes I even went in his office to talk to him. I missed him dearly. If I could have given all this shit up and have him back, I would. Still to this day, I wanted to kill he person that killed him. I was going to find out who did it one day.

When I pulled up, I sat there and looked at the building. My mother had done a good job making sure that it stayed just the way that my father had it. This place was his pride and joy. I rolled me a Backwood while I waited on my brother to arrive. I finished rolling it just as he was pulling up.

"Damn nigga what the fuck you done did now? I just left yo ass," Jim asked when he stepped out the car.

"Mane, Trinity ass walked up on us while we were eating," I informed him.

"I thought you said that you were done fucking with her?"

"That's the point, she wanted to know why I hadn't been answering her. You know that a nigga love Maci, I don't wanna fuck that shit up," I expressed. Just as those words left my mouth, I heard a car pull up behind me. I turned around to see Trinity.

She was nuts and I really did *not* have time for her ass. "Trin, why are you here? What the fuck don't you get?" I angrily asked. She was looking at me like I had said something wrong. "Furthermore, how the fuck did you know where I was at?"

I had once told her about this place, but I had never brought her here. That meant that she had to have followed me. "I rode to you club and didn't see you and I know you said that you and your brother come here sometimes. So, I decide to see if you came here," she informed me. She was looking sad like that shit was going to change the way that I felt. She had the game fucked up. She was never my girl so she had no right to think that she could question me. I didn't feel like I ever made her think that doing that was okay. I could count how many times that I could have taken her out in public. So, what made her think that she was my woman?

"Trinity what the fuck made you think that shit was cool? What the fuck made you think that you could disrespect me or my girl?" I asked. I wanted to know what the fuck she was thinking.

"I love you Reese and if you think that I'm going to just let you be with someone else like I haven't invested my time in you, you're crazy," she said. This bitch had lost her mind.

"What the fuck have you invested in me? All you have done is gave me some pussy," I exclaimed. I needed her to know that shit. I guess I was too damn nice to her. I hit the blunt and passed it back to my brother just as she broke down on the ground crying. I looked at Jim just as he walked off. I started to help her up, but if her dumb ass wanted to be down there, that's just where she was going to be.

I walked off because she was not worth my time. As soon as we walked in the door. I heard glass break. I knew that she had done something to my car, but I didn't care. I just kept walking.

"Mane she fucking yo shit up," Jim said as he look out the small window that was on the door.

"That's cool when she get done I will never fuck with her again and I got plenty damn cars so broke windows in one don't bother me. I will get that shit fixed," I told him as we took a seat at the bar.

I had a million other things to worry about other then them car windows. We ordered food and talked about a few business ventures that we had been working on. After a few hours we both headed home.

12
TRINITY

Reese had me fucked up if he thought that he could just walk away from me like that. He was my man. I had been faithful to this nigga for two years and he thought that he was going to play me like I was a joke. He had me fucked up. There was no way that I would let them be happy. I was going to show him how much I loved him. He was my way out. When I met him, I was good when it came to money, but now my daddy was in a lot of debt, so I needed to keep Reese around. He never really gave me anything, but I knew that he had money. See, I was smart because I didn't ask for shit from him, so when I really needed him, I would be able to ask. I mean, I had other niggas that I fucked with that had money and had no problem giving it to me, but they were not Reese. A part of me loved that nigga. He was different from any nigga that I had fucked with.

Once I busted his window, I waited to see if he would come back out and see what the sound was. I knew that he heard it. After about twenty minutes of waiting, I pulled off. I headed straight to my cousin's house. I had to tell her about this shit. When I pulled up, her boyfriend's car was in the driveway. I hated when he was over because she acted different. She acted like I wanted the nigga or something. What she didn't know was that I had already fucked him. I just decided to go home because I didn't feel like the fake shit. Once I made it in the house, I called this nigga that I had met a while back. He was so fucking fine and paid. From what I had heard, he was in the same tax bracket as Reese.

"Yo what's up lil mama," he cooed as soon as he answered.

"Nothing much, I was just thinking about ya," I lied. I mean I did think about him, but not like I was making it seem.

"Bet, when you gone let a nigga come through?"

"When you ready. I'm just at the house chillin," I told him. I was cool with him coming by because I wanted to fuck. I wanted some dick, so he was going to have to do since Reese was in his feelings.

"Bet, drop yo location. I will call you when I'm headed to you," he said before we ended the call. I jumped up and started cleaning up. It had been a while since I had cleaned up. Reese was the only nigga that really was coming over, but when he stopped coming, I stopped cleaning every day. I had so much to do. After about three hours, I was done. I threw me some chicken in the oven so that we could eat. I knew that was the way to a man's heart.

I walked through the house making sure that everything looked good. Once I was satisfied with how my house looked, I jumped in the shower to make sure that my shit was smelling good. When I got out the shower, I realized that it had been damn near five hours.

Me: hey wyd

901-555-7783: nothing finna head to you

Me: ok

I smiled before throwing my phone on the couch. It didn't take him long to get to me. When he called and said that he was outside, I triple checked the house again before going to the door. There he was rocking some baller shorts with a white tee and Gucci slides. Even though he was dressed simply, he looked like money. I guess the fact that he pulled up in a Range Rover made it look better. Even the way he walked was a turn on. He walked in the door and looked around before nodding his head in approval. That made me smile.

"What's good, ma," he spoke as he hugged me. He smelled so fucking good. And the accent was so sexy on him.

"Nothing much. I'm finna go check on the food. I will be right back," I told him as he took a seat on the couch. While I was in the kitchen, I grabbed my phone so that I could see if Reese had called. When I saw that Reese had, call I kind of got in my feelings.

He ended up joining me in the kitchen. While he rolled his weed, I finished cooking the food. It was like everything about his ass was sexy. I wanted this nigga. I could tell by his walk that his dick was big. I didn't really smoke, but I wanted his ass to like me so I hit it a few times. I fixed our plate when the food finished. We made small talk while we ate.

"So go on and eat me for dessert," he said as he sat his plate on the counter. I hadn't expected him to say that. Now there was no reason that I couldn't have him. While he was standing there, I dropped to my knees. He was wearing joggers, so I was able to get them down quickly. His dick was so fucking pretty. I used my tongue to get the tip wet. I had just finished with my water, so my mouth was cold. He gripped the counter just as I made his dick disappear. I had mastered the whole art of dick sucking. Shit, that was how I was able to get what I wanted out of these niggas. I closed my eye and imagined that he was Reese. Damn, why the fuck was I thinking about Reese when I had this fine ass man in front of me?

I cleared my mind of Reese and focused on making this nigga want to come back. I could tell that I was sucking it just the way that he liked. Rough sex was what I needed, and the way that he was gripping my hair was turning me on.

"Damn baby, suck that dick," He called out as she fucked my face. The way that he was moving had me so wet. I could tell that he was about to nut by the way that he was looking. As soon as he was about to nut, he pulled my head back and nutted all over me. A little landed on my lip, so I licked it off. That must have turned him on because he grabbed me and bent me over the counter.

I knew that he was pulling on a rubber because it took him a second to slide in. I couldn't lie, that shit took my breath away. His shit was big as fuck. He was a little rough, but I wasn't going to complain. I needed this nigga in my life. After we fucked, I went to get him a towel. When I came back to the front of the house, he was on the couch with his dick out. I walked over and cleaned him off.

"So, you got a nigga?" he asked me as I finished up.

"Naw, me and my ex, Reese, on bad terms right now. He was cheating, so I been falling back," I lied. I just didn't need him to think that I was some desperate female that didn't no other nigga want. One thing I learned was that a nigga didn't want a bitch that no other nigga wanted.

"So, how long you and the nigga been fucking off?" he asked as I walked off.

"We been together for three years," I lied again. He didn't reply. When I walked back in the living room, he was on his phone. I sat beside him and he pulled me closer. He had a cool vibe. We ended up laying around talking until he got a call and had to leave.

As soon as he was gone, my mind went right back to Reese. I needed to come up with a way to get him away from her ass. She was brainwashing him and I could not let that happen. He was my man and I refused to let her have him. I had put in too much work for her to come along and think that she was going to have him.

13
KRESHA

"Bitch, get off the phone so that we can get to the shop on time," I told Maci's phone boning ass. Her ass was just mad at the nigga a few days ago, now she back to her regular routine. They stayed on the phone all day. When she wasn't on the phone, they were together. Secretly, I was in my feelings a little. Even when she was with Lee, she always made time for me. Now it felt like I was just her roommate. I could not tell you the last time that we had gone out and had lunch. She had stopped working both jobs and still didn't have time for me. I had been waiting on her today because I would get some alone time with her.

"Baby ima call you back. Let me finish getting ready before she have a heart attack," she told him just as I walked back past. My ass was dressed and ready to go. I had plans to see Jim later. He wanted to take me on a date. It had been so long since I had been on a date. I talked to people here and there but that was about it. For a while, I was scared of what Nell would do if he found out. At this point, I didn't care what he thought or how he felt.

I was done not enjoying life. I just hoped when he came home that he didn't start with his shit because I knew for sure that Jim was not going to back down. While I waited on her, I scrolled on Facebook. I had a few friend-requests. I didn't know any of the people, but I accepted them anyway Just as I was getting up to see what she was doing, she walked in my room. She was dressed so cute.

We gathered everything that we needed and headed out the door. We were still sharing our car. I would be so happy when I got my own car. She mostly drove his cars though. I was happy about that part. I was able to do more. I had enrolled in a networking class, so it was better since I was able to drive to class.

I wanted to get into IT. I loved anything technology centered. I wanted to do something that would take me a long way. I had a few talents, like I was really good at make-up and cooking. I just didn't see myself doing anything like that for the rest of my life. At some point I wanted to open my own staffing agency.

I had big dreams and I was not going to let anyone get in the way of them. I wanted to do so much in life. I knew that this was not the end for me.

We made it to the shop in no time. I was happy that it wasn't packed. I hated to hear all the gossip. It was no one business to tell someone else business. I didn't really care about other people's issues. As soon as we walked in the door, she ushered me to the shampoo bowl. Maci's ass was on the phone as always.

"Girl, you and all this damn hair," Justice my hair stylist, fussed. I had been going to *Hair Justice* salon for the past few years. She was the G.O.A.T when it came to this hair shit. She was my girl, one of the few that I could say that about.

"Who you telling?" I joked just as she sat me up. The shampoo bowl was at the back of the shop, so we were able to see everyone that came in the door. When the door opened, everyone's attention went to the girl who walked in the door.

"What's up, Kay. You can have a seat and I will be with you soon as I shampoo-ing these two," Justice informed her. The girl nodded and took a seat. She finished shampooing me then got started on Maci. Maci's hair was done already so she was just getting a touch up. I was getting a full install. I wanted to make sure that I was looking good for him. As I sat under the dryer another customer came in, only she was for one of the other stylists. From what I observed, she was friends with the Kay girl. I put my headphones in as Maci was lathered with shampoo.

    Jim: wyd
    Me: at the shop getting my hair done
    Jim: Call me when you get done im picking you up
    Me: ok

I smiled just thinking about the fact that I was about to see him. The vibe that we had was so real that nothing could mess it up. He was like my other half. We weren't in a relationship, but he was bae. He made me feel like a queen anytime that he was around. He opened door and all. I was so into the music that I was listening to that I didn't hear Justice call my name. She ended up coming over and getting my attention.

"Damn girl you thick," said the girl that had come in after the Kay girl. I thanked her and walked back to where Justice was. After she spoke to me, I noticed her say something to the Kay girl, but I didn't pay it any mind. One thing I knew for sure was that there was always a hater in the room.

    Mai: girl whats up with them hoes?
    Me: I guess I wasn't wrong
    Mai: hating hoes

That had me on alert, so I decided that I would leave my headphones on, but cut them down. She rinsed the conditioner out then sat me in the chair so that her assistant could dry me and braid me down. I noticed that both girls kept looking at me. I wanted to ask what the fuck they were looking at, but I didn't want to have that drama at Justice's shop.

"Girl, you know Jimbo ass ain't going nowhere," the girl Kay said loud enough for everyone in the shop to hear. Now, it may have been because the music stopped, but I doubt it was that.

Just when she said that, I remembered the second girl from the day that we pulled up on them. She spoke to him.

Mai: oh lord

Me: girlllll

I laughed matter-of-factly. I was not the one to play with.

"I wonder if Reese's fine ass still with Trinity crazy ass," Kayla called out. At this point, they were doing the most. I looked at Maci and she shrugged. I knew that she wasn't bothered. One thing we knew was that Reese's was all hers.

"Make sure you ask Jim. Cause that nigga can get it," I looked at Justice and she just shook her head. These hoes were reaching and just didn't know that I was the one. I had time to break a bitch's face. I wondered who the girl was. I wanted to ask him, but they would be here when he got here, so we would see.

14
KAYLA

I was hot when my girl told me that the same girl that was getting her hair done was the bitch that Jim was with. I didn't know what was up with him. He had been acting stand-offish since that day. He hadn't really been talking to me. He would come by the house to check on Lil Jim, but once he made sure that he was good then he would leave. On the other hand, it was cool because I was able to spend time with Co. It seemed like me and him were getting closer. A part of me hated that I started fucking with Jim's ass.

I was so ready to leave here so that I could roast Jim's ass. I couldn't believe that Ke Ke was not lying. He was really with a bitch. I watched as Justice did her hair. The girl that was with her was done, but she was still sitting near the back. I had to mention Jim because I wanted her to know that he would never stop fucking with me. I had his first child. He will always be mines.

"There go yo baby daddy," KeKe said getting my attention. I looked back to see him walking towards the door with Reese following. My blood boiled as I watched him text on his phone. I had been texting his ass but hadn't gotten a reply at all. He walked in the door right past me. There was no way that he was coming to pick her up. I was so shocked that I couldn't say shit, that was until he kissed her.

"Jim, you lost yo fucking mind!" I yelled, making everyone in the shop look my way. This was a long shot since I knew that he hated drama, especially in public. I didn't care though, he had me fucked up.

"Aw shit what's up Kay?" Reese's fake ass said, causing everyone to laugh but me. I didn't see shit funny. I was doing everything I could to keep the tears from rolling down my face. He had done the same shit to me again. How could he?

"Did you really kiss her?" I asked as if I hadn't just seen that shit with my own eyes. He looked at me like I had done something wrong. I knew that he was mad because I was making a scene, but I didn't give a fuck. He had the right one. I jumped up and rushed over to him. Before I could hit him, his punk ass brother stepped in the way. He couldn't save his ass. I was going to kick both of their asses. They had me fucked up.

"Chill on that ghetto shit, Kayla. You think I don't know about the nigga you been fucking with? You played yourself. Next time, wait until I'm gone before you call the nigga," he said, leaving me stunned. What the fuck did he know? I had been slipping up by answering Co while he was in the house. I would only do it if he was in Lil Jim's room. I knew that if he was there, he was distracted, so he wouldn't be paying attention. How did I let that shit happen?

"I fucking hate you," I yelled before walking out the door. I was so mad and embarrassed. He was going to pay for playing me. See, he thought I was the same Kayla from back in the day, but he had another thing coming. I was going to show his ass.

I jumped in my car and broke down. I knew that I was wrong, but damn he had done the same shit to me twice. Was I to blame? I knew that I could have let Co go, but I cared about him. Hell, I loved the nigga. But I loved Jim more. All he had to do was talk to me and I would have let Co go. Just as I was about to pull off, my phone rang. I saw that it was Ke Ke, so I hit ignore. I didn't have time for the million questions that she was going to ask me. I didn't know the answers.

I buckled my seat belt before pulling off. I headed to my house. The more I drove, the more I realized that I didn't want to be alone. I made a U-turn and headed in the direction of Co's house. As I got closer, I called his phone but didn't get an answer, so I headed back towards my house. I cried the whole way home. I was heartbroken.

Just as I was pulling up at home, Co called. "Hello?" I answered. I was doing my best to hold my cry in. I knew that it would make him mad that I was crying over Jim.

"What's wrong baby?" he questioned in a concerned tone.

"It's just a lot. Can you meet me?" I cried.

"Just meet me at my house" he told me before ending the call. I did a u turn and headed to his house. I went over what I was going to say in my head. I knew that I couldn't tell the truth because he would be mad as fuck. I made it to his house in no time. When I pulled in his driveway, I checked my phone just to see if Jim called to explain. When I saw that I didn't have any missed calls or texts, the hurt became anger.

I waited in my car until Co pulled up. As soon as he cut the car off, he rushed over to me. Just seeing how concerned that he was made me smile. We went in the house, and I told him the made-up story about how he was mean and rude and tried to take my son. Co was just as pissed as I was. He knew how I was about my son. I knew that what I was doing was fucked up, but Jim had brought this on him self.

"Baby don't you know when that nigga make his drops?" Co asked. I sat there for a second. I didn't know if I wanted to get involved in that. Although he hurt me, I didn't want to bring harm to him. There was a chance that the shit could go wrong. It could be all bad. Jim wasn't a punk, and neither was Co.

"I can find out," I lied. I knew that Jim wouldn't want to talk to me. I was going to make him wish that he left me alone. He didn't have to come and make things hard for me. I was good. Now I was going to make shit hard for both him and her. I would just follow him until I figured it out. Either way, his ass was going to pay. I didn't know when he made his drops, but I did know where all of his trap houses were.

15

JIM

Kayla though that a nigga was stupid. I knew that she was fucking with the Co nigga. When I heard her on the phone, I started asking around just to make sure that I was right. I knew that the streets would tell me everything that I needed to know. I just wanted to see how long this shit was gone last. It would have been easy to just ask her about it but who was I kidding she wouldn't have told me the truth. Kayla was a sweet girl and I was good on her. If she wanted that broke ass nigga then she could be with him.

"Who was that?" Kresha asked soon as we got in the car. I really hadn't told her much about my baby mamas because I didn't think that it was that important. They were not her worry.

"That was Lil Jim's mama," I confessed. She nodded her head then adjusted herself in the seat. I really couldn't tell if she was mad or not.

"She's nothing to worry about," I assured her after she picked up her phone. I didn't want her to think that I was going to bring drama in her life. She didn't reply so I just left the shit alone. I had planned to take her shopping, so we headed to the mall.

Kresha's was a natural beauty. My baby was looking good. I

love the way that her hair was. I grabbed her hand causing her to look up at me. There was just something about this girl. I loved the way that she looked at me. It was as if she could see through me or something.

"You mad?"

"Nah." I wanted to ask again to be sure but you decide that I would just leave well enough alone.

It didn't take long for us to get to the mall. When we got there, I valeted the car then helped her out. Once we were done here, I knew that she wouldn't be mad anymore. I helped her out the car and we headed to tear the mall down. Kresha wasn't my girl, but a nigga fucked with her. I could see myself being with her. I made a mental note to see where her head was at when it came to being in a relationship. As much as we were together you would think that we had made shit official, but we had even talked about it at all. I had been gone so maybe this changed. I remember that you had to verbally say that you was in a relationship but that may have changed since I was gone. Maybe I was just old school.

Me and my baby hit damn near every designer store. I had a candle lit dinner planned for us later. I wanted to be the one that made her happy. The vibe that we had was so chill that I wanted it forever. Gucci was the last store that we needed to go in. Soon as we walked in, she stopped walking.

"I don't want anything out of here," she said before turning around and going back out the store. I saw a few people in there but nothing that stood out. I just walked off behind her and made a mental note to ask her about that later. We had been here for a while, so we decided to go and get something to eat to hold us over until dinner. We walked to the food court hand in hand. I knew that she would want fries from Chick-fil-A. That was her favorite. We ordered our food then stood to the side.

"What's up baby daddy," hear from behind me. I turned to see Shae. I hadn't really seen her since I came home. My baby girl was always with my mama or me. She looked bad. Nothing like the woman that I knew. I guess what I had been hearing was the truth and was getting high.

"What's good, Shae?" I spoke as I pulled Kresha closer to me. I wanted Shae to know that she was my girl. I didn't need her saying shit out of line. Kayla had done enough of that.

"Can you give me some money to get Miya some shoes?" she asked. I had to look at her because she couldn't be serious. There was no way that she was serious.

"Shae, if you needed some money, you could have just said that. Why would you lie and say that you were doing something for Miya when she's never with you," I questioned. I wanted to know what made her think that I was going to go for that. She knew better than that. I didn't have shit for her ass. She didn't even care enough to make sure that our daughter was good, and here she was asking me for money. I wanted her to be a good mother to our baby. She needed that. How could she not know that? I guess it was to be expected since her mama wasn't shit.

"Baby, our food is ready," Kresha said as she pulled me away from Shae. I was happy that she did that because I knew that Shae's ass would have kept talking. I held my baby from the back and boy did she smell good. We got our food and headed to the door. When I looked up from talking to her, I saw the CO nigga's brother. His brother and I had beef for years before I left. The nigga was hot about me fucking his bitch. For the life of me, I didn't get why he was still mad about that shit. What that nigga didn't know was that he was beefin' with himself. I was living too good to be beefin' with any nigga. I gave the nigga a head nod before grabbing the food and following her. I could look at his face and see that he was mad. One thing I knew was that they didn't want that smoke.

"I wanna go to Miami," she told me out of the blue. "I have never been there. Shit, I haven't been anywhere really. My ass has been working since I was in high school. It will be nice to enjoy life for a moment."

I just nodded my head. There was no reason to respond because what was understood didn't have to be explained. I was going to give her the world as long as she let me. I looked at the time, and we had a while before dinner, so I decided to head to my mama's house.

"So, what are we doing?' she asked me causing me to take my eyes off the road. I really didn't know what to say. I hadn't really thought much about what we were doing. I was just going with the flow, but I was down for whatever she was down for. I knew that I was just getting out of jail, but I know a real one when I met one.

"Baby, we can do whatever you want to do. A nigga fucks with you, so I didn't feel like it needed to be spoken on. You mine, and I'm yours," I assured her. She just smiled before stuffing her mouth. My baby was even sexy while she ate. Once we were done, we headed to the car. I loved walking behind her. It was something about that walk that had a nigga's head gone.

For the rest of the day, we chilled until it was time for dinner. Just as we finished eating, I got a call from Lou. I guess she could tell that something was wrong because she jumped up before I could. I threw four hundred dollars on the table before we headed to the car.

"You want me to drop you off first?" I asked. I didn't want to but if she wanted me to I would. He said that the trap had been robbed. I didn't want to ask any questions because we were on the phone.

"Naw baby I'm good. Go see what's going on. If I need you, I will call Maci to come and get me," she told me. I just nodded and headed to the trap. I like that she was ready to ride with a nigga. The average female would have wanted me to drop her off.

The whole ride there, all I could think about was who in their right mind would try me like this. My brother had been running this shit while I was gone with no problems. So why did niggas want to try me now. As I drove, she grabbed my hand. That shit calmed me down instantly. I can't lie I was ready to kill a nigga. When I pulled up, I parked in front of the house. It was dark out, so you really could see who was out. I didn't care who was around though? I didn't play about my money. I jumped out with my baby following. When we walked in, Lou was laying on the couch holding his arm. There was a nigga laid out on the floor and one looking like he was barely holding on. I walked over to the guy that was still alive just as my brother walked in the door. Seeing the scene made me even madder than I already was.

"Who sent you lil nigga?" I asked as I leaned over him. He smiled like this shit was a game. It didn't matter to me, he was dying today either way. I pulled out my gun and finished his ass off. I looked at Kresha, and she was just looking. I really didn't want her to see that side of me, but what was done was done. Once again, I couldn't read her thoughts. Her face was blank.

"So you gone act like you can't hear? I questioned.

"He's from the north," she said shocking me. I just looked at her. Hearing her say that had me on alert. When all this was over, I needed to talk to her. She had been on something else today. How the fuck did she know this nigga?

I called the cleanup crew and the doctor. Lou had been shot, but it wasn't anything that he wouldn't live through. The crew was there in no time. As they got started, Lou told me what had gone down. I can't lie I was pissed. A nigga really had tried me. Like why now? Since I had been gone, my brother had been doing this shit, and no one had ever tried us. Shit was running smoothly until now.

While they cleaned, we looked at the cameras. I had to give it to Lou; his little ass was bussing that chopper. He had proven himself for sure. I made a mental note to give him a bonus. That was some real shit. That lil nigga risked his life to protect my shit, and I respected that.

Kresha was falling asleep, so I headed out so I could get my baby home. I knew that she was ready to go. When we got in the car her phone started ringing, she just looked at it and silenced the call. The whole ride I was thinking about how I was going to switch this shit up. I wasn't going to get rid of the house; I was just going to move my shit. They did get away, but I wasn't going to give them and chance to come back. Whoever sent them would be looking for them soon?

We pulled up to her house just as a car was pulling off. That was odd, but she didn't say anything, so neither did I. Her phone rang, and whoever it was she ignored them once again. She had been doing that a lot lately. Whatever it was would come to the light sooner or later. Once we were settled, I laid back in her bed while her head was in my lap.

"So you gone tell me what's going on with you?" I asked. She was normally so open with me, but today had shown me otherwise.

"What you mean baby," she asked sitting up.

"When we walked in the store you saw somebody. Who did you see?" I questioned. She dropped her head, and I can't lie, that shit had me worried. It was something about the look on her face that didn't sit well with me.

"I didn't want to tell you this because I did want to run you away. My last relationship ended badly. When I was seventeen, I met this guy name Nell. At the time I thought that he was everything I needed. That was until he knew that he had me. It went from verbal abuse to physical. About two years ago, he came home one day and told me that he had a baby on the way. I tried leaving, and he damn near beat me to death. My dumb ass still didn't leave. I stayed, and that was the worst thing I could have ever done. It was like the beatings got worse. He would beat my ass for anything. I could cough, and he would beat my ass. He ended up going to jail for robbery and when he did, I used that as my opportunity to get away. I am either at work or home. I did that to make sure I didn't run into anyone that he knew.

When we walked in Gucci, I saw his brother. I just didn't want him to see me with you. I didn't want to bring that drama to your life," she explained. I pulled her close to me because I needed her to hear me loud and clear.

"Baby you don't have to worry about me. As long as I'm around you don't have to worry about anything happening to you. Baby, I'm that nigga and I don't fear a soul, so while we are together, you better not fear a soul." That shit had me hot. One thing fa sho that nigga was gone have to see before he could touch her.

"Is that who's been calling you?"

"Yes," she replied holding her head down. I grabbed her head and forced her to look at me. There was no way that I was going to allow her to feel bad about a nigga doing her wrong. I hated niggas like that. As a man you know that you can't beat a female's ass. That's some real pussy shit. If a female makes you that mad, then get away from her. I got a mother, and I know that I would flip the fuck out if a nigga hit her.

I pulled her to me and kissed her. I wanted her to know that I was her protector. I would always make sure that she was good as long as she was with me. That was my job as her man. She pulled back and then kissed me again. That shit had a nigga dick rock hard. She made her way to the bottom of the bed and slid my dick in her mouth. Her mouth was warm as fuck. That shit had me ready to nut just that fast.

"Shit baby," I moaned out as she deep throated my dick. Her sex game was crazy. She made sure that I was drained each and every time. Since we had been fucking, I didn't have the desire to fuck anyone else. She made sure that she sucked the soul out a nigga. She had a nigga toes curling and all.

"Come here," I demanded. I couldn't take that shit anymore. She climbed on top of me. It was something about looking at her while she rode my dick. She had this thing that she did that drove me crazy.

"Ummmm baby you feel so good inside of me," she moaned

out. Her voice was so sexy. I can't lie a nigga was in love. I just didn't want to tell her that and run her away. Shit we had just made sense.

"Nut all over that dick," I told her as she rode me slowly. She started moving faster, and that shit had me nutting all in her. I knew for sure that she was going to be pregnant soon because all we did was fuck. I didn't want any more kids but shit it's whatever. Hopefully, she was on some birth control.

Once we finished, she climbed beside me and fell straight to sleep. This was when I wished that I was at home because I would have been in my office. I slid out of bed and grabbed her laptop. There were a few things that I could do from here. I was wide awake and needed to do something to ease my mind. I wanted to know who the fuck tried me, and I knew that I wouldn't be able to sleep until I found out. I logged into the camera system. I wanted to see the few days before just to see if anyone had been watching us. My brother had cameras on the house and down the street. So we could see everything that was going on. I played the videos on mute, but I wanted to hear them. I headed to the room that they used as an office. After listening to the tapes I called Lou.

"What's good," he answered.

"The female that came over that day. Is she yo baby mama?" I asked.

"Nah, Just a lil female that I bust down here and there. Why you ask?"

"She was in the car with the nigga a few days ago. I can see on the camera where the nigga you killed dropped her off around the corner," I told him. He didn't say shit for a minute.

"I'm finna call her up. Can y'all meet me at the trap?" he asked. He needed to chill. We would handle it later. I could tell that he was pissed by his tone, but there was a time and place for everything.

"Nah, let's sit on it on it. Get well because shit gone be different from now on. A nigga respect what you did today.

When you are well, we are moving you to another position," I advised. He didn't reply, but I knew that he would appreciate it. "I will come through tomorrow so we can talk." After we ended the call, I looked at a few more things. As I closed out what I was doing, a folder on her desktop caught my attention. I opened it and wished that I hadn't. The folder was pictures of her after he attacked her. That shit damn near brought tears to a nigga eyes. How you do that to someone that you claim to love? I was gone kill that nigga.

Just as I was getting ready to go to the room, my phone rang. It was after midnight, so I had no idea why Kayla was calling me. She had made her bed now, she was going to have to lay in it. I was done with her. She was fucking with the OPPs, and that was a no go for me. I hit ignore and headed back to the room. All I wanted to do was lay down with my woman.

16

REESE

I don't know what made these niggas think that it was cool to play with me or my money, but they gone learn today. I hated a nigga that didn't have the drive to get their own money but was ready to try and take some shit.

After my brother left, I started counting so that I could take the money with me. I called a few of the workers so that we could move the dope from here. There was no way that I was going to ride with it. Shit, that was what they were for. I was glad that we had a solid team. They always did what was needed and stayed out the way. None of them were flashy and loud, and I was grateful for that. We had six spots total.

I laid back on the couch and tried my best to relax. I needed to come up with something because I knew Jim's ass was gone be on one in the morning. I puzzled my mind about who I trusted enough to have at this spot. I knew that it had to be someone that was about their money. I pulled out my phone and called Lo. Currently, he was running one of the other houses, but I knew that he would be good over here. He didn't have kids or a bitch that I knew of, so he could be here for the late nights.

"Yo," he answered.

"Come through," I told him.

"Bet," was all he said before ending the call. Since I was alone, I decide to Facetime my baby.

Maci had a nigga wide open. There wasn't a day that I went without seeing her pretty face. She was all a nigga needed and wanted. She had shown a nigga what it was to have someone love them. She catered to a nigga. I don't see how her ex could mess up what he had, but I was happy that he did because if not, she wouldn't be mine.

"Hey, baby? Everything good?" she asked. I knew that she was concerned, but I was good. I was with her when I got the call.

"Yea, I'm going to stay here tonight. I don't want to leave it unattended," I told her. She just looked at me.

"What that look mean?" I questioned. I really didn't know what she was thinking, so I just laughed. Since we had made shit official, she didn't like sleeping without a nigga, and I can't lie I felt the same way.

"I'm on the way," was all she said before hanging up. I just shook my head. I knew that she was not going to let me sleep alone. I chilled until she called and said that she was pulling up on the street. She always did that. She told me that she didn't want anyone to try anything.

I walked to the door to meet her, and I could have sworn that I saw Trinity's car. She had still been calling my ass all day every day. I didn't see why she didn't get the picture. She had been leaving notes on my car and all kinds of shit.

"Hey baby," she greeted me as she looked around. I just pulled her in the house.

"Why were you looking around like that?" I asked. She had been doing that for a while. I just hadn't thought to say anything about it.

"I been feeling like somebody has been following me," she informed me. When she said that, it made me think about the other day when we went to dinner, and I felt the same way. I knew that it had to be Trinity's crazy ass. I hated to say it, but I was going to have to kill her ass. She was doing too much about a nigga that was not hers. I let her slide when she fucked my car up, but now, she was pushing it.

"We good baby," I assured her. She placed her bag down and sat on the couch. Since she was no longer working, she had started smoking so she picked up the blunt that I had rolled and lit it. It was sexy seeing her like this. I love the plain Jane Maci much better than the Maci that was always dressed up. I just sat there admiring her. I had no idea why she wore makeup her skin was perfect. Maci was everything a nigga wanted. Just as I relaxed her phone rang. She looked at it and hit ignore. She had been doing that a lot lately. I knew that it was probably her ex calling.

"Who was that?" I asked. I wanted to see if she was going to lie to me.

"That's Lee calling," she said as if it was nothing. I wanted to question her more, but I decided against that. I wasn't insecure at all, so the fact that she wasn't answering for him was enough for me. Just as I was about to reply, we heard a loud crash. We both jumped up and run to the door. Soon as my eyes landed on Maci's car, my body filled with anger.

"What the fuck?" she said running out the door. Good thing that she was parked on the street. Otherwise, my shit would have been burned up too. Just as I was about to pull her back into the house, I saw Trinity's car. Soon as I looked that way, she pulled off. I can't explain the anger that I felt as my baby cried. I knew that she had worked hard for her car. Getting her another one was no issue. It was just the principle. We didn't have to call the fire department because one of the neighbors had already done it. I was pissed because I didn't need the police coming over here. We sat on the porch and watched them put the fire out. Once that was done, we talked to the police. I didn't want to talk to them, but I knew that I didn't have a choice. Soon as they were gone, I called and had someone come and stay the night. I wanted to be in my own bed. My boy Lo came like an hour later. Soon as I made sure that he was good, we headed to the house.

The whole way to the house I was thinking about how Trinity really played me. I couldn't wait to pull up on her ass. I knew that she was going to act dumb, but I knew her car. Some shit I just didn't understand. Like why you would do some shit like that? Why run up behind a nigga that clearly showed you that he didn't want you. I hadn't ever done anything to make her think that I wanted to be with her. I always treated her as a fuck. I never spent the night, nor have I ever let her come to my house.

By the time that we made it to the house, it was after four in the morning. All I wanted to do was lay down. A nigga was tired. When we walked in the house, Maci went to the bedroom, and I headed to my office. There were a few things I wanted to look at. I was starting to think that it was her that was following us. As I watched the video footage rage filled my body. She had been just sitting outside my house. That was some creepy ass shit. I hadn't seen anything like it. Once I had seen enough, I headed to shower.

When I walked in the room, Maci was standing at the mirror. I stood by the bed watching her. She was so into fixing them long as lashes that she didn't see me. Maci was perfect. The way that her ass was eating up the shorts that she was wear had a nigga dick rock hard.

"There you go with that," she smiled. I already got the shower going for you." See, it was the small shit like that that made me love her. I walked over to her and kissed her before going in the bathroom. My baby had all my shit laid out. I don't see how a nigga could fuck up something so good. I undressed and jumped in the shower. While I showered, I thought about all the plans that I had. I wanted to get out of the streets. Shit, I wanted both me and my brother to get out. I made a mental note to talk to Jim to see what he thought about letting Lou run shit. He had proven himself and we were millionaires so there was no reason that we should be touching anything.

After I brushed my teeth, I headed to lay down. Maci was laying in the bed on her phone. I was more than sure that she was reading. Soon as I got in the bed, she locked her phone and laid it down.

"If you could get any car, what kind would it be?" I inquired. I had to replace her car because, in my eyes, it was my fault that Trinity had set her car on fire. Plus, I knew that she and Kresha shared that car. Getting her a car was number one on my agenda tomorrow.

"A Porsche truck, or a Range Rover," she advised. I hated Range Rovers, so Porsche it was. I really wanted to have the Lambo truck, but I also wanted her to have what she wanted. I pulled up my phone and texted my guy at the car lot.

As I looked down at her beautiful face, I could help but kiss her. It was something about the way her soft lips felt on mines. I couldn't help but feel that she was what I had been missing in my life. I felt complete. I knew that we had started fucking off, but I felt something with her I never felt before. Besides that my mother loved her. Hell, they talked more than we talked. Maci was going to be my wife sooner than later.

17
MACI

THE NEXT DAY

"Which one you like better?" Reese asked as we look around the two Porsche trucks. I can't lie my ass was overwhelmed. I had never really shopped for a car. The car that I had was what I could get at the time, so I didn't have to look. But here I was walking around this car lot with all these cars that cost more than I made in a year. Reese was literally upgrading my life. Now, if I could just get Lee to leave me alone, I would be good. It seemed like he was just fucking with me. I had blocked every number that he called from. I counted the other day, and so far, I had blocked thirty-two numbers.

"That one," I pointed at a back Benz truck. It wasn't one of the ones that he was showing us, but Reese said that I could have whatever I wanted, and I wanted that one.

"Let's go look to make sure it's what you want," Reese told me before grabbing my hand. I followed behind him. Soon as he opened the door, I knew that it was the truck for me. It looked like his truck just newer.

"Oh my God baby, I love this truck." I cooed. When I looked up, he was standing back smiling so big. He and the salesman walked off, so I decide to call Kresha.

"What's up bitch," she beamed. I was loving the new Kresha. Jim had my cousin glowing. She was so happy with him.

"So, bitch look at our new whip." She was so heartbroken when I told her about the car. I didn't work anymore, but she still did, so that was her means of transportation.

"No ma'am that's yours this is mines," she said before turning the camera around. Jim had gotten her a new Benz coupe.

"We are twinning bihhhhhhh," she screamed. I didn't have my air Pods in, so everyone in the room looked my way. I just shrugged because they didn't get the joy that we felt. Me and all my bitches were riding Benz's. I could wait to show my aunt. I knew that she was going to be happy for the both of us. She deserved to be happy after what Nell put her though.

I looked up to see that Reese needed me. "Ima call you when we leave here," I told her before ending the call. When I made it to the office that they were in Reese pull out the chair for me. The guy started walking me through the paperwork. I was so happy that it was in my name. Not to say that he would have tried to take the truck, but you know shit happens. An hour or so later, I was headed home in my new 2021 Mercedes GLE53 Coupe. I couldn't be any happier.

When I pulled up at the house I sighed because Lee's car was parked across from my house. I didn't get why he was still trying. As I approached the house, I decided to just keep going because I didn't have time for his shit. I wanted to enjoy this moment, and I was not about to let him fuck it up for me. I just headed to Reese's house.

On the way, I stopped to get something to cook. I knew that it was going to be a while before he made it home. I decide to cook Steak, parmesan potatoes, and asparagus. I wanted to show him my appreciation. I had the biggest smile on my face as I walked through the store. That was until I hit the corner and spotted Lee walking towards me. There was no way that he was here.

"So you gone keep ignoring a nigga," he damn near yelled. He was doing the most. First off, we were probably the only black people in the store, and then he had the nerve to be loud. That was not a good combination at all. I just kept walking in hopes that he would keep going about his business. "I guess you thought I didn't see you when you passed your house. Baby, I told you I'm sorry. Now you need to forgive a nigga so we can move on." This nigga had to be smoking crack or something. There was no getting back together.

"Lee, why can't you just leave me alone?" I questioned. He was doing to fuck much at this point.

"Baby you need to stop acting like this something new. You knew that I was fucking with other bitches," he dumbly said.

"You gotta be on drugs if you think that shit cool. I didn't know shit. I loved you so I forgave you. That was not giving you the ok to keep doing that shit. You made me kill my baby just so that you could go have a baby with someone else. I will never forgive you for that. Now leave me alone," I yelled before leaving the basket and walking off. I rushed to my car in hopes that he wouldn't follow me. I just wanted to go to my man house and cook him a meal. Just as I was closing my truck door Lee grabbed it.

"So you think I'm going to let you just be happy with that nigga?" I knew from the jump that he would never do that. That was too much like right.

"Lee, you don't want me you just don't want anyone else to have me. I have moved on and you should do the same." Before he had a chance to reply Reese pulled up. I was so happy that he did because I knew that Lee would just let me go.

"Aye go find some safe to do my nigga," Reese called out soon as he was close to us. That took Lee's attention off me. I closed my car door started my truck.

Lee just nodded and walked off. I sat there just looking crazy because I didn't know what to say to him. I hadn't really seen him this mad. I let the window down and he just walked off. I shrugged and waited until I saw Lee pull off. I guess having a good day was out the window.

18

KAYLA

A FEW DAYS LATER

"So did you find out anything?" Co asked soon as I walked in his house. I just rolled my eyes because that was the first thing that he asked anytime he saw me. Since I had seen him with ole girl, he hadn't been answering my calls. I hadn't seen him either because Lil Jim had been with his mother. So there was no way for me to find out anything. He was getting on my nerves. Hell he did even ask me how my day was or shit. All he talked about was Jim's ass. I hated that shit.

"Naw I'm going to find out what I can when I pick my son later," I told him as I headed to use the bathroom. I needed to figure this shit out because I didn't want anything to happen to Jim. I knew that he was the one that was providing for me and my son. Co was so adamite about doing this. I had no idea what he had against my son father but clearly the hate ran deep.

I was in a bad position. I loved Jim but I was in love with Co. I kind of hated myself because I knew better than to get involved with Jim. Nothing had changed about him. He could have easily talked to me about Co. After I finished using the bathroom, I headed to see what Co was doing. I couldn't find him, so I looked outside and saw that he was gone. I grabbed my phone called him. That was out the normal for him he always gave me the heads up. I called him but didn't get any answer. I just grabbed my shit, locked up and headed home. There was no reason for me to be here if he wasn't here.

Ring Ring

As I was driving KeKe name flashed across my radio. I really didn't want to talk to her ass. I let the voice mail catch it, but she called back, so I answered.

"What's up?'

"Damn bitch you answered like I did something to you. I was just calling to check on you."

"Girl my bad. Co ass done pissed me off." I expressed. I wanted to tell her what was going on, but I didn't know if I could trust her ass. She was always telling me other people's business so I knew that she would have no issue telling someone mines.

"What his ass do now?" she inquired. I was quiet for a second because I was thinking.

"Just meet me at my house," I told her. I needed to talk to somebody about this. I could have talked to my cousin Trinity, but she was so in love with Reese that I'm sure that she would tell his ass. I don't get how she was in love with a nigga that would never be with her the crazy part is she knew that he would never fuck with her. He had told her a million times. Hell, I heard that he was in a relationship now.

We ended the call as a pulled in my driveway. I sat there for a second because I realize how much Jim had done for me. I needed to really think about what I was doing. Would Co make sure that I was good the way that Jim had? Hell, even when he was with Shae and when he was in jail, he made sure that all my bills were paid. I can't tell you the last time that I had paid any bills. See this was why I needed to someone to think through this with me.

Luckily, I had already cleaned up. I grabbed a bottle of wine and put it in the fridge. I knew that she didn't really drink liquor. I flopped down on the couch and unlocked my phone. I needed to pay my rent. Just as I finished with that, the doorbell rang. I opened the door because I knew that it was KeKe. I was shocked to see that it was Co, especially since he had left and didn't tell me shit. I just walked off and went to my room.

Me: the door open

KeKe: ok almost there

I didn't want her to have to wait for me to come to the door. He closed the door as if someone else was in the house. I sat on the bed so that I could see what he had to say.

"Where the nigga live? And don't say that you don't know."

"I been told you that I didn't know because I drop my son off at his mama's house," I lied. There was no way that I would tell him where Jim lived.

"Ok where that's at?" I just looked at his ass because she had to have been out of his mind. His mama didn't have anything to do with the beef that they had. Not only that my son and Miya was there so why would I put they life in danger like that. The more that I was around him I was starting to not like him. How could you want to do something to an old lady?

"Co my baby is at her house there is no way I can tell you that," I honestly told him. He just nodded and walked out the room. When I made it back to the living room, KeKe was on the couch scrolling in her phone. I knew that I told her to come over, but I really did want to talk now.

"So what was that about?" she asked as I flopped down. I just wished that I could go back in time. I wouldn't have fucked with Jim. I know that he's not to blame but he hurt me. And as you know hurt people hurt people. I needed to think of how I was going to get out of this shit. I knew that Co was not going to let this shit go.

"Girl he want me to help him set Jim and Reese up," She just looked at me. Her face was scrunched up so knew what she was thinking. One thing I knew she was going to tell me the truth nit just what I wanted to hear.

"You gotta be dumb. Girl Jim the one that take care of yo ass. What has Co done other than fuck you to make you want to do some shit like that. I never once heard you say that nigga did anything for you or yo child but you ready to risk it all for a nigga that won't do it for you. What happens when Jim finds out you are helping him. You and I both know that he will kill both of yall. What about yo baby? What if he gets hurt in the process? I heard him ask about Jim's mama house. That lady has done nothing but be good to you," she fussed. I didn't think about all of that. I was just thinking about how Jim hurt me.

"I did think about all of that," I admitted.

"I know you didn't because all you was thinking about was him hurting you when you was never doing right from the jump. Yea he was fucking with somebody else but so were you."

I just dropped my head because she was right. Now I had gotten myself in some shit that I didn't know if I could get out of.

19
TRINITY

I had been sitting outside Reese house for the past three hours praying that I could catch him without her. I was tired but I knew that I needed to stay awake. I was waiting in her ass to leave. It seemed that lately they had been together a lot. She hadn't even been going to work. Why did she need to be under him like that? She was living the life that I was supposed be living. He was my man first. I was going to get him back one way or another.

I had devoted my life to following them around. I can't tell you how hurt that I was when I saw him getting her a new truck. That should have been my truck. When I burned her shit up, I just knew that would run her away but it just made them closer. At this point I didn't know what to do. He was never alone. Either he was with her, his brother or his fine ass cousin. The one day that I thought he was alone he when to his mother house. That was another thing I didn't like. I had known him three years and I never meet his mother, but she had in a few months. What was it about her that made him do all of this stuff? I mean I was the total package. What more did he need?

Just as I was getting ready to just go home the garage lifted. A smile graced my face as I watched him place a bag in the trunk and jumped in the driver seat. When he pulled off, I waited for a second and then I pulled off behind him. I made sure that I kept a safe distance. As we approached his club I pulled to the side. I wanted to give him time to get in there. I was happy that it was mid-day because that meant that it was no security there. After about twenty minutes I check in the mirror to make sure that I was looking good before making my way to the door. The door was unlocked so I walked right in. There were people doing construction.

No one was paying attention to me, so I made my way to his office. I stood there for a second to see if he was on the phone. When I did hear any talking, I grabbed the doorknob and slowly pushed the door open. As I walked in the office, I cut my camera on. I sat my purse and phone down making sure that the phone was facing the desk. I was so smooth with it that he did notice what I was doing. He was sitting at his desk looking good as fuck.

"Yo why you here?" he asked with looking my way. I wanted him to look at me, so that he could see how good I was looking.

"I can show you how much I miss you," I explained as I made my way to his desk. I knew that I was looking and smelling good so there was no way that he couldn't resist me. As I got closer, I untied my shirt making my big perky breast pop put. I watched as he adjusted himself.

"Trinity, I told you I got a girl now," he admitted as I dropped to my knees. I wanted to taste him. I needed to, hell.

"I won't tell if you don't tell," I assured him. If I couldn't be his girl then I would be his side bitch either I was going to be in his life. Before he had a chance to stop me, I pulled his dick out of the sweatpants that he was wearing. I slowly licked the head just how he liked it. I smile on the inside as I watched him throw his head back. I knew then that I had him.

"Shit I miss this head," he moaned as he grabbed a hand full of my hair. I had just gotten my shit done but I didn't care because it was him. If it would have been any other nigga I would have stopped. He was fucking my face hard, and that shit had my pussy dripping wet. He pulled my head back before getting up and opening the drawer. I just stood there waiting for him to grace my life with that big ass dick that he was toting around. I watched as he placed the rubber over his dick.

"Turn around and don't make a fucking sound," he demanded. I did as I was told. Baby he took my damn breath away. I wanted to moan out so bad, but I knew that he means what he said about making a sound. I bit down on my bottom lip so that I wouldn't moan out. He was fucking me so good. I came at least twice before he started moving faster letting me know that he was getting ready to nut.

Soon as he pulled out, I stood up and faced him. I could read his face, so I walked over to my purse and grabbed my wipes. Just as I was putting my phone in my bag, he waked up and grabbed it. My goddamn heart was beating so fast. "Next time you wanna try and record me make sure do I better job hiding it," he said as he went through my phone and deleted the video. He handed me my phone before walking over to the same office.

Just as I was getting ready to walk away. He grabbed me by my neck. I damn near pissed on myself. "Don't come near my girl or her car again," he gritted. When he let me go, I lost my balance and fell in the floor. "And don't call me if I wanna talk I will call you," he added before opening the office door for me to leave. I got up and left. As I was walking out the door his girl walked in. I just smiled and kept going. I could tell that she was wondering who I was. I didn't care as long as I was in his life, I was good.

20

REESE

Trinity was playing a cold game. She knew what she was doing. The fucked-up thing is I knew too, and I still took that chance. Especially since I knew that my girl was coming up here. I just prayed that they didn't run into each other. It was something about the way that she sucked dick that a nigga loved. Now don't get me wrong Maci sucked a mean dick, but Trinity would let a nigga nut all in her face and shit. I could never do that to my woman. I looked at the time and saw that I had about twenty minutes before Maci got here. She was coming by to take care of a few things since I had hired her as the Marketing director. She was handling all of my marketing needs for all of my businesses. If it were up to me, she could sit at home and spend my money, but my baby wanted to work so I made it happen. I was cool with it. I just didn't want her working for anyone. She was with a boss, so it was only right that she became one.

"Why was she here," Maci questioned soon as she walked in the office.

"I don't know. I didn't ask I just sent her ass back out the door," I lied. She didn't reply she just nodded her head before placing her laptop bag down. I knew that she didn't believe me, but she left it alone. I sat at my desk and damn near had a heart attack. The rubber paper was on the floor under my desk. I was really slipping. I did my best to slide it all the way under so that she couldn't see it. I could tell that she was mad. I pulled her to me and kissed her on the neck. I knew that I could fuck her, but I needed to take her mind off Trinity.

"Let me show you what I came up with," she said as she pulled away from me. I watch as she pulled her laptop out. I used that time to pick up the wrapper and slip it in my pocket. I would throw it away when she left. Today she was dressed in some Nike tights with the matching crop top and them shorts had that ass sitting up just right.

She walked me though what she had done, and I had to say that I was proud of my baby. I knew that she was going to take this place to a new level, and I was ready. Once she was done, she packed her shit up. I could tell that she was still mad, but I was going to fix that.

"Come here," I demanded pulling her in my lap. "I miss yo pretty ass.

"Umm I guess." I softly brushed my finger over her pussy and just like I thought she was wet as hell. I kissed her on the neck causing a chill to go through her body. I made her stand up and pulled her pants down then had her to sit on the desk.

I knew that I had to get that attitude out of her, and I knew just how to do that. I flicked my togue across her clit making her moan out in pleasure. I loved pleasing her. I never ate a female ass until her. She brought a side out I didn't know I had. I licked and sucked on her until she cum. Once I was done all she could do is lay back panting.

"Why that pussy always taste so good," I asked causing her to smile.

"I wanna go to Ruth Chris and I want some new shoes," she said as if I would give her the world.

"Gone make the reservation and use the card I gave you to order the shoes baby," I told her. I knew that would make her forget but it would do for now.

21
JIM

"Baby can you get me these?" Kresha asked turning her phone towards me. She was showing me some Gucci slides. She was sitting on my lap even though no one was on the couch but us. Hell, no one was in the house but us. I wasn't used to that, but I loved it. My baby loved being under me.

I lifted her so that I could get my wallet out of my pocket and handed it to her. "Which one, baby?' she questioned.

"Any one that you want." She shrugged and pulled out a card. I can't lie; she was easy to satisfy. She didn't ask for much. Most of the stuff I just bought she didn't have to ask. Once she was done, she put the card back and sat the wallet on the table.

"Maci, can I have some ice cream," Lil Jim asked as he jumped on the couch. Anytime that she was here, he didn't ask me for anything he was always calling on her.

"Come on baby,' she said grabbing his hand. She was so attentive to my kids. They loved her as much as I did. Miya ended up coming into the living and seeing him with the ice cream, so of course she wanted some. We all sat on the couch eating ice cream and watching tv. This was life. I couldn't ask for more. God had really blessed me. There may not be a nigga that can go through what I went through and come out on top like I did. I was able to make sure that my family was good, and that's all I could ask for.

"Ok Lil Jim go and take your shower and Miya, you go and get your hair stuff," Maci instructed. The kids got up and did as they were told. While they were gone, I pulled her close to me. I love her scent. Just as I was about to kiss her my phone rang. It was my baby mama Kayla. I hadn't really talked to her since the day that I saw her at the shop. She had been calling Lil Jim on his phone.

"Yea," I answered.

"I wanted to see if you had anything planned for lil Jim tomorrow. If not, I was going to come and get him and take him to a party."

"That's cool. Just let me know what time," I told her.

"Ok," was all she said before ending the call. That was a weird call. Her tone seemed off, but that was not my bitch to be worried about. I could believe that she played with me like I was a sucka. She knew that I was known, so I was going to find out what she was doing. When I came home and asked her was she fucking with anybody, and she told me that she wasn't. She could have been real and told me the truth.

Then she was fucking with a nigga that did like me, so that made the shit worst. I knew that she did know everything was going on, but I'm sure the nigga had said something. He was a snake in my eyes, so was she. I know that she felt that I was wrong, but I wasn't because I wasn't really fucking with Kresha, but she had a whole relationship going on.

Since Kresha was doing Miya's hair I decided to go to my office and get some shit done. My brother had sent me the marketing strategies that Maci had put together. When I walked into my office and logged in to my computer, I saw that I had a Facebook notification. I saw that it was from KeKe's crazy ass. I fucked with KeKe because she was real. She used to fuck with Lo back in the day. I have no idea what happen with them. All I know she don't fuck with that nigga at all.

I didn't want to be talking to her while Kresha was here, so I didn't open the message. I would get up with her when I got out. I had plans to meet my brother to do the count and move some shit around. We normally did re-up for our traps at night. There was less movement during that time. Since the shit that happened the other day, I wanted to make some changes. That situation just showed us that someone was always watching. We let Lou work the warehouse and had replaced his spot with someone else.

"Goodnight, daddy," Miya said as she jumped on the couch that was on the other side of the room. I looked at the time because I knew that it wasn't late.

"Why you going to sleep so early?"

"Because my mommy said that she's coming to see me," she explained. She had to have called her from her brother's phone because I know I hadn't called. If Kresha called, she would have told me.

"Aw ok, when you talk to her?"

"Jim called for me," she admitted. I made a mental note to tell him to ask me first. I knew that Shae was too busy running the streets, and there was no way that she was going to make time to be a mother. That was too much like right.

Shae had changed so much while I was gone. She was nothing like this before I left. It seemed that she was ready for me to come home so that she could run the streets. Being a mother was the last thing that she was thinking about. At first, I was mad that she just said fuck my baby, but I would rather her be here than there with her. She had been with me for the past two months. Not one time did Shae ask about her, and I saw her all the time. I was ashamed to say that she was my baby mama.

"How about we go to the mall tomorrow, and if your mommy calls, I will take you to see her."

"Ok, Daddy," she nodded in agreement. I may have been a

little biased, but my Miya was the sweetest little girl. Her smile always brightened up my day. I couldn't ask for a better daughter. I ended up cutting the TV on for her so that she could watch a movie while I worked. I knew that she was going to fall asleep. By the time that I was done, she was knocked out. I picked her up and took her to her room, then headed to see what my son was doing. When I walked into his room, he was playing the game as usual. He was so into the game that he didn't even notice that I was in the room. I closed the door and headed to shower and throw some clothes on so that I could get in the streets. Just as I was walking in my room, I heard a loud crash. I rush the table in the hallway and grabbed my gun that I kept there. I had them motherfuckers all over the house. I never knew what was coming my way.

As I made my way down the stairs, I saw a shadow. The way the house was made I couldn't see who it was. Kresha had already cut everything off down there, so it was almost completely dark, aside from the kitchen light. Soon as I hit the bottom stair, I saw the shadow again. I made my way around the wall fired my gun. I couldn't believe this shit. No one knew where I lived but family, so who the fuck was in my shit. The nigga fired back then it was like shots started ringing out. My heart dropped when I heard Kresha scream. I started hitting lights. I needed to lay eyes on whoever was in my shit. When I made it to the kitchen, Kresha was laid out on the floor.

"Daddy," Lil Jim cried. When I looked up and saw a nigga at the top of the stairs holding my son by his shirt. My heart dropped. How this fuck did I let this happen? Just as I turned to make my way to the nigga that was holding my son, a shot went off and everything went black.

www.ingramcontent.com/pod-product-compliance
Lightning Source LLC
LaVergne TN
LVHW042301261224
799977LV00032B/443